FORCED IN BETWEEN

First edition published in October 2019 by Crystal Peake Publisher

Print I S B N 978-1-912948-02-4
eBook I S B N 978-1-912948-03-1

A catalogue copy of this book is available from the British Library.

Typeset by Crystal Peake Publisher
Cover designed by GermanCreative

Visit www.crystalpeake.co.uk for any further information.

Alexandra Ispas

FORCED IN BETWEEN

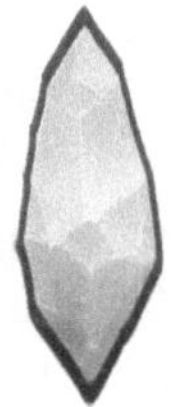

Crystal Peake Publisher
www.crystalpeake.co.uk

CONTENTS

1
Where it all begins

I can't go on like this. I just can't.

***

Jennifer, a teenage girl, had been living a harsh life. For as long as she could remember, she lived her life among men. How the world reached this state was a mystery to her and all of humankind, as far as she knew. Nobody would tell her how she was brought up on this planet everyone seemed to call 'Earth', or to what purpose. All she knew was that she had to move on and get used to it.

Ask no questions, ask no questions, she would tell herself. *Asking useless questions makes you weak, and that's the last thing I need.* Living under stressful circumstances, she never expected to see the light of another day. *Always expect the worst.*

FORCED IN BETWEEN

If you're prepared for that, you're prepared for anything.

Being the only girl in the world may seem abnormal, but Jennifer was used to this lifestyle of living among men only. Training every day so that none could exploit her weaknesses has made her almost invulnerable.

The world had been suffering a horrible war against alien invaders who were trying to take over their planet, putting everybody's life in peril. The war continued for decades and all women had been mysteriously disappearing ever since. That is, until Jennifer. All men treated her as a weak and useless child, simply because she was not a man herself.

She had to prove them wrong somehow, and this war was the perfect opportunity... unless it killed her.

***

'Don't let them get in, or else we're doomed! Fortify all entry ways so they don't infiltrate through our numbers, and push their assault from the main hall and out of our settlement. Make sure none of them reach the laboratory. We need no spies lurking all over the place and discovering our advanced technology. Now go, sergeant!'

'Sir, yes sir!'

The noise was getting louder, and the danger was increasing by the second. They were approaching. Alien forces were marching towards their well-secured settlement which was looking more like army grounds. Advanced technology had led them to this; as wonderful and as incredible as technology may be, it comes with a price. One which could leave a grave scar on the history of the world. This was war.

'What will you have me do, commander?' asked someone, with a softer voice compared to all others. It couldn't be one of the soldiers, yet the person was seeking to help in the war.

'I already told you, Jen, stay in your room. You'll be safe there.'

'Why can't I help to? I'm as good a fighter as anyone here. I'm fearless, I'm strong enough to carry whatever weapon you lend me. My aim is perfect, and need I remind you that I have more practice than most around here?'

'Jen, it's an order. Go to your room right this instant!'

'Give me a good reason and I will.'

'Stubborn kid. Fine, I'll give you your reason. You are a girl. Now move along, go!'

'If that's what you think, then fine! When the world starts falling apart because you wouldn't let me help you, you'll find me in my headquarters.' And with those words she left, slamming the door shut behind her.

She quickened her pace until she started running like mad. *Don't cry, just don't cry, or they'll say you're weak again.* Tears were flooding her eyes, but she wouldn't let it show no matter what.

In a couple of minutes, she reached her headquarters, slammed the door shut like she did earlier and threw herself head first on the bed.

Why won't he let me help? So, what if I'm a girl? Why would that matter? He said it as if he only meant to mock her; calling her a kid and reminding her that she's not a man, something she'll never be. *I wish they wouldn't see me like that.* The words the commander had just said echoed in Jennifer's head over and over again, until she eventually fell asleep to the sound of explosions and gun shots outside.

You are a girl... a girl... a girl... But don't worry Jen, you'll show them one day that you're more than that, and they'll regret all the pain they put you through. One day they're going to pay.

2

Fight to your last breath

Everything went silent. The war wasn't over yet, but the alien forces must have fled.

The silence was deafening now. Everybody was used to the loud noise and the adrenaline of fighting for one's life.

Jennifer was still sleeping, and sleeping heavily too. Eventually she woke up, though with a bit of help from her trainer.

'Late for class again! Wake up, kid!' he muttered as he threw a bucket of ice-cold water over her face to wake her up. Instantly, she rose to her feet, shivering. Was it the cold water or the fear of her trainer?

'Next time I find you late for training, I won't even bother to come and wake you up from your slumber. Now on your feet and to the training grounds!'

'You needn't throw that bucket you know! I would've

woken up by other means as well.'

'Other means you say? I'll ask the colonel whether I can borrow some of his venomous snakes. Or maybe scorpions would do?'

'That's not what I had in mind...'

'Silence! To the training grounds with you.'

Gee, why do they have to be so mean? They could at least once be reasonable.

Jennifer kept walking, her trainer right behind her, watching her every move. *Stay straight, don't trip, keep your head high, watch everyone and everything closely and be ready for anything.* Poor Jennifer's mind was a mess, as she thought of everything at once. She was struggling to survive among men crippled by war.

Her trainer was so close that she could hear his breath, slow and steady... and mad. He was so tall and rigid that she always thought he might just get hold of her and swallow her whole at any second.

Something wasn't right though. He never used to walk along so close to her. He must've been really mad this morning, or maybe she was just walking too slow. She started moving faster, almost at a jogging pace, and she heard her trainer close behind give out a sigh of relief.

A couple of minutes later, they reached the training grounds. A part of the training grounds anyway. They sat in a huge room which was full of machinery, exercise mats, all sorts of accessories you could possibly need, and even training for duels, whether be they with weapons or your own body. For someone who enjoyed working out, this place was heaven, but for Jennifer this felt like hell.

Torture time, she thought, just like every morning at 7 a.m. 'So, what's on the list first?'

'Jen, just start with a warm-up. Make sure to make it right and thorough this time, we don't need you going to hospital again because you didn't warm up well.' It was true. She *did* end up in hospital with a strain because she hurried with her warm-up. 'I'll put you in a fist fight against Peter later, so you'd better be careful.'

Oh no! I'm so dead this time! Peter was one of the strongest guys she trained with. He was a couple of years older than her. His shoulders were wide, and his muscles were so worked out that you'd cower just at the sight of him. He rarely had mercy, even for her as a girl. Even so, when they weren't training, he was a true friend to her; one of the few people she could rely on.

I bet that Trainer Blockhead picked Peter on purpose to fist fight me. He really loves to see me lose. That's what Jennifer called her trainer, 'Blockhead', even though his actual name was Breightad. Everyone he was close to -meaning important people, like the commander- called him Tad. Jennifer would never get to call him that without being severely punished. Luckily for her, she didn't even want to.

Warmed-up and ready for a tough fight, Jennifer stepped in the fighting circle where Peter was already waiting, looking doubtful at her. His look almost said "I'll take you as easy as Blockhead is gonna let me.'

'Three...' Blockhead started counting. 'Two...' He would be watching them. 'One...' Watching intently. 'Fight!'

Jennifer let Peter make the first move. As he rushed to hit her, she was able to dodge him by a millimetre, and pushed him from behind, making him fall. *If you aren't as strong as them, use their own strength against them.* He got up quickly, and neared her slowly. *What's he up to?*

Before she knew it, Peter hit her in the stomach, and she fell to her knees. *He hits hard.* Trying to ignore the pain, she grabbed both his feet, pushing them together so that he'd lose his balance. As much as she tried, his position wouldn't allow it because his feet were a good distance away from each other. That's when she tried raising just one of them, and it worked.

His heavy body fell to the ground again, but this time, he fell over Jennifer. The poor girl felt squashed between the floor and Peter. *Why does he have to be so heavy?* As much as she struggled, she couldn't break free. For a couple of seconds, she just stayed there because Peter wouldn't budge. *He must be enjoying his time on top of me, I guess.*

While stuck there, she caught a glimpse of Blockhead watching from the side, rolling his eyes. Further away, there was a group of guys who were watching the fight, and giggling as one of them said something. Obviously, they were talking about how silly they looked fighting.

'This is supposed to be a fist fight, so get up and stop playing!' roared Blockhead, obviously mad at the unexpected outcome of the fight. Still, it wasn't over.

As soon as Blockhead finished his sentence, Peter jumped on his feet, and quickly grabbed Jennifer by the waist, throwing her to the other side of the circle. By the time she could react, he was already next to her on one knee, ready to punch her in the face. *Don't, just don't!* But he couldn't hear her, and even if he could, he wouldn't have faltered anyway. Immediately, Jennifer turned to her side and was surprised to find that she was still whole. Instead of punching her in the face, Peter grabbed hold of her brown-reddish hair, which was slightly longer than shoulder length, making it a great weakness for her in combat.

Jennifer tried to rise up, but Peter pulled her hair downwards and she fell back on the ground, banging her head. Peter was looking right at her from above, still holding the edges of her hair. His expression was of a brute, so mean and merciless you would've run away if you could, but his eyes were pleading for forgiveness. Jennifer saw that crystal clear.

'Stop playing and fight, kids!' Blockhead was raging again, but then he let out a sigh and spoke again. 'Who am I kidding? You're worthless. Stop the fight immediately,' he said, disappointed. He then muttered under his breath, 'You can't even put up a fight. You can't even hit a girl.'

Jennifer and Peter were relieved that the fight ended so easily this time.

'Thanks, Peter,' she said. 'I really thought I'd end up in hospital again.' Her words made him giggle a little.

'Couldn't let that happen again. You're bruised enough as it is. Still, I didn't let you off *that* easy though. You put up a great fight. I liked your first dodge by the way. Didn't see that coming.'

'Really? I mean, are you serious?' *Don't blush, girl. Don't. Blush!*

'Alright, alright,' Blockhead joined in. *Oh no! I can bet on the whole alien army that we're in trouble.* 'What was that, kids? Jen, you did better than I expected, but still worse than you should have,' he took a break and let out another sigh. *Better than he expected? How low are his expectations anyway?!* 'Peter, about you... I'll just tell you this, try to be *real* next time.' He turned his back to us as he finished talking, and I could sense him rolling his eyes. From a bigger distance, he shouted at them. 'Don't forget to keep training, I have got more coming up for you today.'

Jennifer and Peter suddenly started laughing loudly, trying to make sure that Blockhead wouldn't hear.

'Thanks again, Peter. I really owe you this one!'

'It's nothing. I didn't want to fight anyway. Blockhead's been forcing me all morning. I may not show it, but I'm exhausted.'

'He hates us.'

'He does, indeed.'

'Especially me,' quickly added the girl.

'I hate to admit it Jenny, but I think you're right. He hates everyone, but you're the first on his list.' As he said those words, Jennifer looked down, once more upset that she was treated differently only because she was a girl. Instead of apologising, Peter just hugged her sympathetically. She let her head fall on his shoulder, and stayed like that for a minute before realising they had work to do.

Don't cry. Whatever you do, just don't cry, even though it hurts.

'Better get back to work, before Blockhead sees we're wasting his precious time.'

'I agree.'

3

Fighting your brother is never a good idea

The rest of the day went on as slowly as possible. *I thought it would never end.*

After her fight with Peter, they went to practice their swordsmanship. When Blockhead noticed how well Jennifer was doing, he immediately put her up against Mark. Mark was the most experienced swordsman in her year.

He was a year older than Jennifer. Everybody made fun of him, that his cute face and skinny body weren't fit for a fighter, therefore he worked harder than everyone to prove them all wrong. *I'll one day do exactly what he did; I'll prove them all wrong about what I can do.* However, once he started a duel, nothing else mattered. His cute face faded, and he did whatever was possible to thrive. That's how he won all duels for the last few months.

Jennifer had no chance against him, even though she

handled the sword quite well, she lost. Like expected, he always had the upper hand. Still, she focused on staying safe, parrying and dodging most of his attacks, not attacking herself. Even so, she ended up having a little cut on her right cheek and a few even smaller scratches on her left hand and back. Luckily, the one on the cheek was the deepest, and it didn't bleed much, saving Jennifer a lot of trouble... and blood.

After that, she continued to practice on her own and with her friends - who were few - avoiding duels and fist fights for the rest of the day. Blockhead must've got bored of her always losing, so he practically ignored her for the rest of the day. *What a relief.*

Once they could leave the training grounds at noon, they could do whatever they wanted, including staying there a little more - something nobody sane did. Normally she would've gone directly to her headquarters, but this time she changed destination.

'Hey Jenny, wait up!' called Peter behind her, running to catch up. 'Wanna go for a walk with Mark, Nico and I?' Nico was Mark's older brother, by three years. He was a very good swordsman too. Unlike his brother, Nico's mind often drifted away when least expected, making him lose his concentration and get in trouble. Or end up in hospital.

'Sure, why not,' she said smiling. 'Where are the MN brothers?' That's what she called them as a group.

'They're still behind. I ran as fast as I could to catch up with you. You left quicker than Mark's reflexes in a duel.' That made both of them laugh because everybody knows that Mark's reflexes were incredible, better than anyone's, and being told that you moved faster than that really meant something.

'Alright,' she said while placing herself on the floor with crossed legs. 'Let's wait for them.'

Peter did the same, staying next to her, almost touching her. Whether he did or not, Jennifer wouldn't have noticed because she was paying attention to when the boys were going to arrive, looking away from Peter.

'How much longer do you think they're gonna take getting here?' she asked.

'A couple of minutes maybe. They seemed exhausted when I came running for you earlier. Anyway, you put up a great fight earlier.'

'You told me already,' she quickly answered, still not looking his way.

'Eh... I meant the swordfight. You're a great swordsman... swordswoman, excuse me,' he said half laughing, but Jennifer didn't even smile.

'You saw that?! I was horrible!' she said obviously disappointed by her performance, looking now at the floor. Peter then put a hand around her, trying to comfort her. Whether it worked or not remained a mystery, as the girl didn't even flinch.

'Hey Jen!' someone shouted from a distance. It was Mark's voice for sure. 'Look, I'm sorry for the scratches from earlier...' then he noticed Peter next to her, his hand around her still. Mark immediately gave him the what-do-you-think-you-are-doing look, making Peter take his hand back, and stand up. The girl faltered for a second until she realised what happened while she was still looking down. Finally, she looked up, and saw Mark lend her a hand to help her stand. In the corner of her eye, Jennifer noticed that Peter frowned when he saw Mark acting so generously, but his face went back to normal quickly.

'Nico is still on his way, typical him. He's so lazy... oh wait, here he comes,' Mark said, astonished.

'Hi...Jen...I heard that...you've had a tough day...' he said between breaths. He must've been exhausted.

'Nico, are you OK? Your face is red.'

'He's OK, don't worry about him,' intervened Mark. 'He doesn't belong in a gym, like us. He's something of a lab rat,' taunted Mark, trying to annoy his brother. Unfortunately for him, Nico was too busy gasping for air to mind his words.

'Alright, so where do you guys want to go?' asked Jennifer.

'Anywhere you want to, Jen.' They all seemed to agree to that.

'Well... where could we go?'

'What place haven't you seen in like forever?' asked Peter, very eager to get this little piece of information out of her.

'Let's see... other than the gym, everywhere! No, wait, I know where I really want to go,' she said, taking a long break to make the three boys more and more curious.

'Tell us!' demanded Mark.

'Outside.'

They all fell silent.

'You mean...you...you haven't been outside for a long time? How long exactly?' asked Mark, obviously shocked.

'A couple of weeks, maybe a month... I never keep track of time, you know that!'

Returning to reality, Peter added, 'OK then, outside it is.

We're going outside!'

'Lead the way Peter! You seem most anxious about it,' said Jennifer letting out a small giggle. *Why are they all looking at me like that?*

Mark seemed disappointed that Jennifer didn't pick him to lead the way, but then he suddenly became happy when he noticed he was walking alongside her. He couldn't just keep his happiness to himself, and looked her way and smiled. When she turned to look, he pretended like nothing happened. *What's wrong with these two freaks? They're acting so strange today,* she thought.

Trying to hide her confusion, she added with a half laughing, half joking tone, 'why are you smiling like that?' and immediately Peter looked back, frowning.

'Erm... because we're going outside? I'm happy. Am I not allowed to be happy?'

'Taking into consideration we're at war with aliens, I don't think there's much to be happy about right now,' added Nico.

'You saddo, you really belong in a lab. Sometimes I wonder how you manage to even get to the gym. It's a very long way. How come your legs didn't break yet?' Mark went on insulting his brother in the most creative ways he could muster, until Jennifer broke in.

'Enough Mark! I get it that you're brothers and that you sometimes joke like this, but you're going too far now!' When Jennifer was annoyed with someone, it was never a good sign. Mark preferred to stay safe, not confront her wrath. He lowered his head in defeat, and was sorry for making her mad.

'Jenny's right, you shouldn't have...'

'He got it, Peter!'

'I'm sorry.' He lowered his head too.

'Gee, Jen. Sometimes I'm starting to think you're worse that Blockhead!' said Nico.

Mark's eyes were burning upon hearing those words, and he immediately turned to look at his brother. If looks could kill, Nico would've been ashes by now. 'What did you say?' It was almost like time stopped. Mark was shooting killing looks at his brother so bad that you could almost imagine a circle of fire around him, and he was ready to jump on his prey like a human-devouring monster.

'I...I was just joking.'

But it was too late to make him understand, for Mark was already charging at Nico. Mark grabbed him by the neck, and pushed him against the wall, creating a loud thud. Before anything worse happened, Jennifer put a hand on Mark's shoulder and pulled him back so he'd let Nico go, and maybe even fall. It turned out he didn't fall, but he loosened his grip on his brother's neck, and eventually let go of him.

'I...I'm so sorry, Jen. I'm really, really sorry,' he said, trying to hide the tears that were coming. No tears fell, but his eyes were sparkling and begging for mercy. 'I...I don't know what happened. I just got mad and over-reacted.'

Jennifer didn't say a word, but it was obvious that she was disappointed, and shocked. Before any of them could say another word, she just started running down the hallway, trying to get away. *Something's been seriously wrong with these guys lately.*

'Look what you did!' screamed Peter.

'It wasn't my fault! Nico said she's worse than Blockhead. I couldn't just ignore that!'

'Neither could I, but I wouldn't have killed him for saying that! I recognise a joke when I hear it, unlike you.'

As the two of them continued fighting, Nico was laying on the floor, gasping for air. His hands were around his neck trying to protect it, doing everything he could to ease the pain. Eventually the two of them stopped arguing when Mark said, 'This is pointless. We'd better go find Jen quickly and apologise for everything.'

'Trying to catch up with her is useless. We all know she's the fastest runner around here. Plus, she's got a huge head start.'

'We could still try. And besides, we know where she went.'

'Where, smarty?' said Peter mockingly. In return Mark just shot him a look, and ignored his comment.

'Outside.'

And off they went, running as fast as possible to find Jennifer. Poor Nico was still lying on the ground, gasping for air, so he couldn't join the two boys' endeavour to find the girl.

She was the only girl around; how hard could it be to find her?

4

Between hammer and anvil

'I think that's her right there!' one of the boys shouted, pointing in the direction of some flowerbeds.

'We're looking for a girl. How many girls have you seen around other than her?' Peter was right, but Mark simply ignored him and approached the figure that was standing next to the flower beds.

'Jen! Jen, come here!' he waved, but she stood there motionless, like a statue. 'Look, if you're mad at us, fine, I'll take the whole blame if that makes you feel better. But you have to understand we're very sorry.'

'We?' whispered Peter. 'Don't involve me in your mess. It is actually your fault that this happened, so you'd better take the blame on your own.'

'Shush!'

'What for? She can't even hear us.' Again, Mark just

ignored Peter.

When the boys noticed she wouldn't budge, they went over. Waiting for her to come was useless, as she wouldn't even turn around to see them.

With every step, the grass was crushed under their heavy bodies, leaving signs all over the lawn. When they reached her, Peter tried to put his hand on her shoulder to let her know they were there, but his hand went right through.

'Oh no, she's a ghost! What have I done?' screamed Mark, horrified at the sight.

'It's called a hologram, smarty. Look, she left this little device on the ground, and it projects her image crystal clear. She tricked us.'

'So, she's not dead. Phew.' Peter rolled his eyes. 'So, what now?' asked Mark. 'I had no idea she had such devices with her. Makes me wonder where she got them...but anyway, what does this mean?'

'I didn't know she had this either. Anyway, she wouldn't leave a hologram anywhere for nothing. My guess is that she doesn't want to see us...I mean see *you*, after what you did earlier, and I don't blame her.'

'Humph, yeah sure, always blame me for everything. It's not like you're perfect and never did anything wrong in your life.'

Peter sighed. 'Just quit it. We have to find Jenny. That's our priority right now, not fighting among ourselves.'

'I hate to admit it, but you're right this time. Well, I don't know about you, but I'm checking her headquarters. See you later.'

'I'll be looking around here. She might be just hiding.

Maybe spying...'

'Whatever, I'm just glad I don't have to see your face anymore for now.'

'Same.'

***

Seriously, what's wrong with them? They've both been acting very strangely lately. They used to be very good friends before... what could've changed them?

Jennifer was hiding behind a corner, close to the flower bed where she had left the hologram. She did trick them well, and made them look like fools, trying to talk to a hologram. Also, like Peter had guessed, she was spying on them. Now that they went separate ways, there was no point in spying anymore.

Now it was time for hiding.

Jennifer was still outside, in a beautiful garden in front of the Warband Academy, where trainees like her and her friends lived and learned everything they knew. Peter was still looking for her, but in the opposite corner of the garden. He wouldn't find her for a while, but still she wouldn't take any chances. She had to get to her room anyway.

She forgot that she had left the door unlocked in the rush of waking up that morning, and couldn't let Mark just go in. He'd make a mess out of everything!

She had to hurry.

Peter had his back to Jennifer, so this was the perfect chance to get inside without being seen. She started sprinting towards the entrance, but heard her name being called right as she opened the door. She looked back, and saw Peter running up to her. Jennifer pretended she didn't hear or see him coming, and went inside quickly.

I have to get there before Mark does. Luckily, she knew a shortcut, but Peter was following her, almost catching up. She couldn't run any faster because she was exhausted, but neither did she lower her pace. *Run, girl, run!*

As she ran through the long corridors, taking the shortest path to her room, she passed lots of men who looked at her curiously when they saw her running that fast right past them. Luckily for her, she was thin and swift, unlike Peter, whose shoulders were broad. He found it hard to slip though the crowd like she did. This slowed him down a lot, but wouldn't stop him.

Finally, she reached the corridor where her room was, but she saw Mark right in front of her door, knocking with power, making echoes throughout the whole corridor. *Oh well, at least he's got manners and doesn't just open the door.* Still, if he did try the handle, he'd notice the door was unlocked and would've entered, but that never happened. As he turned his head to the left, he saw Jennifer.

The girl quickly cowered behind the corner, hiding. *He couldn't have seen me, right?* she thought.

'Jen? Is that you?' *Darn it, he saw me. Stay silent, girl. Don't move.*

She would've run back the way she came, but Peter was coming that way, and meeting him on the way wasn't exactly what she had in mind. She was stuck between hammer and anvil.

Eventually, both of the boys reached her, and looked at her as though she was a ghost. 'Jen, are you OK?' they asked in unison.

'I just need some peace. I'm confused!' she said, putting her hands on her head, as if her head hurt. Perhaps it did.

'What are you confused about?' asked Peter with a concerned look on his face.

'I don't know...everything.' They didn't say anything, but looked at her in doubt. She sighed, then added, 'You two are making me confused, alright?'

'Us? What did we do?' asked Mark as if he didn't know already.

'You've been acting...differently than usual.' She looked down. 'I need to get some sleep. Now if you'll excuse me...'

'You're right, you need your sleep,' said Mark, obviously caring for her well-being.

Before she left, Mark gave her a big hug, and while doing so, he whispered so just she would hear, 'I'm very, very, very sorry for what I did earlier. I take all the blame for that, and you have my word it won't happen again.' She smiled, the faintest of smiles, but still she smiled. Peter was looking almost furious, but hid his emotions under a mask of skin.

'Oh, Jenny, I just remembered,' said Peter. 'You left a hologram outside. Here, have it back,' he kindly said, sketching a smile, and lending her a coin-sized device in the shape of a very flat cone.

'Thanks Peter,' she said trying to smile, then she left for her room without saying another word.

The boys sat there watching her walk away, and only left

when they couldn't see her anymore, sadness showing on their faces.

5

Hologram gone missing

'Keep your guard up, don't let him get too close or you're done for! Always wait for him to attack, then attack yourself. Look at his every twitch to anticipate his next move. This way you'll find it easier to dodge or block his attacks!' Blockhead was shouting his instructions to Jennifer while she was participating in another duel, but this time not with Mark. It was with some other boy she was training with called Zack.

Mark was there too, just a little further away, leaning against the wall, talking to Peter. They were both watching the girl thrive in the duel, and whispering so that none would hear.

'She's doing great, don't you think?' asked Mark. 'Still not better than me of course, but very well still!'

'I agree to the first part. Anyway, she looks very tired. Good thing it's almost noon, we can get out of this place soon.'

'Right, can't wait.'

'So shall we invite Jenny somewhere today?' asked Peter, keeping his hopes up.

'I'm not so sure about that. She seems exhausted. I'd love to spend some more time with her...and you since you'll obviously be there too...but for her own sake, I'd have her get some rest.'

'You really care for her, don't you?' asked Peter, letting out a big sigh.

'More than myself...but don't tell her. How about you? I noticed you have become extra caring yourself lately.'

'Same as you I dare say...but don't you tell her either, else I'll be having your guts for dinner.'

'Don't need to be barbaric. We both share this feeling... anyway, we should just hope that Nico won't say anything about that. I'll have to keep a close eye on him.'

'Talking about Nico, where is he?' added Peter.

'Haven't seen him since breakfast...he's bound to be around here. No one, I mean *no one* escapes Blockhead's wrath.'

'You're right, let's look for him.'

And off they went, looking for Mark's brother around the training hall, but they couldn't find him anywhere. Jennifer's duel eventually ended, and Blockhead congratulated her for making progress. This was something new for her. Afterwards, they went separate ways. Jennifer was heading for the exit, leaving a couple of minutes earlier, and Blockhead seeming to be looking for something, or maybe someone.

So were the two boys.

The training hall was still quite crowded, but people had started to leave which made it much easier to find whatever you were looking for. Eventually, Blockhead went up to Peter and Mark, but before he had the chance to say anything, Mark started talking.

'Um...hello sir. Have you seen my brother, Nico?'

'Nico? No, not today, young swordsman.'

'What?! He hasn't been here today?' exclaimed Mark, he started to swear under his breath until he saw Blockhead raising an eyebrow at him. He must've been in a good mood today considering how calm he was. 'I'm sorry, I didn't mean to...anyway, so where is he, sir?'

'He asked me for permission to spend a day in the Warband Academy's Laboratory, with all our scientists. He seemed very excited when I granted him permission. I expected you to know this though.'

'No sir. He didn't tell me anything about that.'

'Anyway... Mark, Peter, I've been looking for you.'

'Have you? What for, sir?' asked Peter, obviously surprised. Peter was laughing inside because of how formal Mark was talking to Blockhead. He was doing everything he could to not burst out laughing.

'Our scientists have lost something of value. It's small, a coin-sized device in the shape of a cone. It is meant to create holograms. It has a very high value, as we're using these devices in our war against the Alien Forces, and that one was the prototype. It's needed to create more of them and to make improvements for future versions.'

The two boys listened with their eyes wide open, obviously surprised Blockhead was telling them such a thing. They were clearly both thinking of the same thing. *Let it not be Jen who took it, let it not be her.* As much as they tried to deny it, they knew there was no other explanation.

'So my point is, if you find the device, or the person who most probably stole it, report to me immediately!' The boys nodded, shocked and not daring to say a single word for fear of saying something wrong. 'You're dismissed.'

'Goodbye, sir,' said the two in unison, with shivering voices, as they raced for the exit.

Once they were out of earshot, they slowed down and started talking, looking more serious than ever.

'What are we going to do? We can't let Blockhead down in *this* matter because it's very important for all of us, but I won't just tell him who has it,' said Mark with a very worried look on his face.

'I'm thinking of something,' answered Peter with an obvious frown on his face. 'What if she got it by accident?'

'If it was an accident, I'm sure she would have returned it.'

'It must be another one. I'm sure the scientists created more, and she probably just found one and kept it. Someone else might have the one we're looking for!' Peter seemed excited that he was probably right. Mark was looking at him confused, not sure how to tell him he's completely wrong.

'Peter, do you know what a prototype is?' He nodded. 'Then you should know that there aren't many prototypes created. That might actually be the only one, plus that it's also working, so it's clearly the one we're looking for.'

At those words, Peter lowered his head in defeat, trying to accept the truth. Still, he denied it, and thought of any other possibility which implied that Jennifer wasn't involved after all.

'But, but, but...maybe she built her own hologram...'

'You know very well it's improbable that she did that,' said Mark, finding it hard to see the bright side of things.

Even so, things were about to get worse, as Blockhead was standing right behind them, with a confused look. 'Are you boys talking about Jennifer?'

'We are...no, no we're not actually...we were just...she... erm...'

'What about her, Mark? Tell me right away!' he said, still looking quite calm, but he could've exploded in anger any second now. When the boys remained silent, he added, 'I expected you to be discussing the matter about the hologram.'

'We were actually,' said Peter quickly, not so sure he did the right thing.

'Didn't you say you were talking about Jennifer?' he inquired, suspicious.

'We were, but...we...um, changed the subject?' said Mark, trying to find a good excuse for talking both about Jennifer and the hologram, but couldn't find anything that would be believable. Of course, Blockhead wouldn't believe even that much, so the boys sighed in defeat, and Mark went on, saying, 'we think she might have it, but we're not sure yet.'

'Jennifer? She has the device? Where is she?' demanded Blockhead, almost showing his frustration, yet also a little relief. Did he want her to have taken the device, or was he just glad it was found so fast?

'She most probably went to sleep. After all, she did look exhausted after training today.'

'Come, we need to check.'

'Yes, sir,' they said in unison, and left right away.

On the way, Mark asked, 'and what if she's sleeping? I don't think we should wake her up.'

'I'll use it as an excuse for her being forty-two seconds late for training yesterday.'

'That's harsh…eh, I meant…'

'I know it's harsh, but it's better than nothing. I need to keep you, young folk, on high alert all the time. You know very well we're at war. I don't want to start this story again, you already know it, so let's just get moving.'

'Yes, sir,' they said in unison once more.

After a while of awkwardly walking along the corridors of the Warband Academy, the three of them reached Jennifer's room, and knocked on the door. There was no answer, just like the two boys expected. Still, Blockhead wouldn't give up, he continued to knock on the door, harder and harder.

'Um, sir? I don't think it's helping. Maybe she's not even there.'

That's when Blockhead tried the handle. The door was locked. She was either hiding inside, or she locked it and went somewhere else. But where could she go? Outside?

It seemed that the two boys were thinking the same thing as they briefly nodded in agreement without whispering a single word. Still, before they went to look for her, they had to get rid of Blockhead. They couldn't afford to have him there when they explained the matter to Jennifer.

'Blo…sir,' started Peter, choosing his words with as much care as possible. He tried again. 'Sir, I'm sure you're going to see Jenny tomorrow morning anyway, so I don't think you need to rush things at the moment. In case we see her, we're certainly going to tell her to come see you, isn't that right Mark?' he said, turning his attention to his friend.

'Yes, of course!'

'Alright guys, you convinced me. Keep in mind that the sooner we get that prototype back, the better it will be for all of us.' And finally, he left while the boys were still standing next to Jennifer's door.

'Alright, time to go look for her.'

'I sure hope we find her quick!'

6

The Vengeful One

'Look, there she is!'

'Peter, that's the hologram again.'

The two boys were standing on the grass outside, looking at Jennifer's figure which was now crouched, legs crossed, looking away from them. As the two of them approached her, she didn't even flinch. Just as Mark suspected, it was a hologram again.

'What do we do now?' asked Peter in confusion. 'I bet she's hiding from us again, but I can't figure out why.'

'If she doesn't want to see us, I won't force her. I respect her privacy and so should you. Now let's take the device and return it to the lab.'

'You think it's the best idea? We should at least let Jenny know about it.'

'We can explain later. For now, we have to do what's right,

I know she'll understand.' Mark paused and sighed. 'She would have done the same, I'm sure.'

'Ok, but if she gets angry, you can take the blame,' demanded Peter.

'Like always.'

***

What are these freaks up to? They're stealing my hologram!

Jennifer was spying on the boys behind a corner, wondering what they were up to this time. She was too far to hear what they were talking about, but she could clearly see they were stealing her hologram.

The girl let out a sigh. There is nothing she can do right now, so she might as well return to her room and get some rest. All of the training that day had exhausted her. The good part was that she was getting better and better, and even Blockhead had started to encourage her for once.

Still thinking of the events that day, she walked towards her room, watching as everyone went by in the other direction. People who didn't know her always looked at her in confusion, because she was the only girl around. She got used to it and learned to ignore them.

When she got to the corridor where her room was, she noticed someone was standing right in front of her door. At first, her instincts told her it was either Mark or Peter, or in the worst case, even Blockhead.

She was wrong though.

Zack, the guy she had her last swordfight with that day, was leaning against the door.

He was tall and strong, but sometimes clumsy. You could see the confusion in his eyes sometimes, and he was always staring at his nose. Probably because it was so big.

The girl cautiously approached him, trying to figure out his intentions.

'Zack?' she asked.

'Jennifer, you finally came.'

'Why were you waiting for me?'

He didn't answer directly, but instead he pushed her against the wall, and looked down at her, frowning.

'I know what you're trying to do,' he said.

Jennifer tried to stay calm as she looked up at him and quietly asked, 'What?'

'You know what I'm talking about. You're trying to gain Breightad's favour by being the best at everything, you little Miss Perfect. Well, I assure you that it won't happen for as long as I am here to stop it,' he said in a growl, hitting the wall with his fist. Zack missed her head by a millimetre. She didn't make a move though, not even blink.

*I'm not afraid of this guy. But I could play innocent at any point if I wanted...*she thought.

'I really don't know what you're talking about, but it doesn't matter. You're very good yourself in pretty much everything, so don't worry about me. All I'm doing is trying to survive.' And with those words she walked away from him, unlocking the door and getting in without saying another word.

Quickly she locked the door so Zack wouldn't be able to get in. That guy could be dangerous.

FORCED IN BETWEEN

***

'Who's that?' whispered Mark, hiding behind the corner with Peter.

'I bet that's Zack, the guy Jenny defeated in a swordfight today, remember?' answered Peter, whispering just the same.

'Oh yeah, it's him alright. I smell trouble here. This guy is a vengeful one. I hope Jen's ok.'

'I'm sure she is. She can take care of herself.'

Zack was still in the corridor, looking at Jennifer's door in confusion as if it were some masterpiece he couldn't decipher. Only a minute later he woke up from his daydreams and went along the hallway, minding his own business. Unfortunately, he went towards the two boys. When he saw them, he snorted and frowned at them, and then left them behind without a word.

When there was bigger distance between Zack and the two boys, Peter said, 'We have to go and talk to Jenny to see what Zack's problem is. And the hologram too.'

'You're right. By the way, since you brought up the hologram. We still have to return it to the lab. Give it to me, and I'll have Nico make sure it gets in the right place. After all, he's gonna be going to the lab tomorrow for sure.'

'Good idea. Here, take it.'

Mark took the device and put it in one of his pockets with caution not to break it or lose it. It was his to hold on to for the moment, until he could give it to Nico who would return it once and for all.

'Let's get some rest too. There's no way Jenny's going to come out of her room anytime soon,' suggested Peter, and Mark nodded in agreement.

The boys took one more look down the corridor to check Jennifer's door. They then let out a sigh and parted ways.

7

Two Freaks, One Girl

The following day, Jennifer, Mark and Peter went to training as usual, and as Mark expected, Nico went to the lab again. Fortunately, all of them finished at the same time, so they could see each other if they wanted to.

During training, Blockhead's mood was unclear, so he didn't shout as much. Even so, the three kids managed to get out with a couple of bruises or cuts; in Jennifer's case, both.

Leaving the training hall exhausted as usual, Jennifer sneaked out first, with a suspicious look on her face, so they tried to follow her. Unfortunately for them, Blockhead noticed them trying to get out a few minutes earlier, so he stopped them.

'Gee, that girl is a lucky one,' whispered Peter, Mark nodded in agreement.

This time they wouldn't find out where she went. Could

it be outside again? Directly to her room? They wondered. However, her destination was somewhere else, and only she knew it. She was going to get her hologram back one way or another. She was heading for the lab.

Strange odours hung in the air, giving her the needed clue that she was getting close.

Running at full speed, she turned around a corner, and was surprised to find herself on the floor with a headache. She bumped into Nico, who was wearing glasses and a lab coat.

Both of them stood up, and Jennifer tried to pass him before he could stop her, but it was too late. The boy caught her arm, and asked where she was going.

'I, uh... have an appointment!'

'What appointment? Are you going to see the dentist, or do you need some surgery done?'

'Um...I need to see to these cuts...they're worse than you might think.'

'Then you bumped into the right person, let me have a look,' he said, with a strange smile on his face. She quickly took her arm back saying 'no'.

'What? Why not?'

'Because...I already have an appointment!' she shouted, and the two fell silent. The boy let out a sigh, and added:

'Jennifer, I know you're up to something. Tell me, what is it?'

The girl sighed and placed herself on the floor. 'It's a long story, we might as well sit down,' so he sat down next to her, eager to find out what this was all about.

'Go on, start your story,' he said.

'Well, forget the story. The point is I'm trying to get something back from the lab.'

'Get something back from the lab? Don't you know that what's in the lab, remains in the lab?'

'But it was stolen from me!'

'Ok, ok, no need to shout. So, what is this thing that was stolen?'

'It's a little device,' she said, showing with her hands the size, 'which can make holograms.'

When he heard those words, Nico's heart skipped a beat in astonishment. The girl looked at him confused. Quickly he said:

'Jennifer, what you're talking about is the H4K, which is currently a prototype, and you can't have it back. Mark actually asked me to return it to the lab this morning, and I had no idea where he got it from. He didn't mention it had been in your possession.'

'But...but it was mine! I just found it lying on the ground one day. And you know what they say, 'finders keepers'...'

'Jennifer, you must understand that you can't have that back,' he told her, raising his tone a little, so she sighed in defeat and looked down. Before anything else happened, Nico added: 'So let me get this straight. You lost your H4K and thought it was in the lab, so you just wanted to get inside and hope it was the first thing you'd see?'

'I...I couldn't make up a plan...'

'You could have asked me.'

'How was I supposed to know you'd be here? Nobody told me!'

'Doesn't matter, now you know. Just keep in mind that from now on, instead of training at the gym, I'll be in the lab.'

'Sure. I hope you're having a good time here.'

'Oh, I am! Much better than with those barbarians who don't know anything else but fight, fight, fight!' At his words, she started giggling. Nico joined in to with a more powerful laughter.

Eventually, Jennifer broke the laughter with a sigh when she remembered that she wanted to ask Nico something. Before she could say anything, the boy looked at her in confusion.

'Nico, I wanted to ask you something. It's about your brother...and Peter...'

'Those two freaks? What about them?'

'I don't know for sure, but I think they're starting to act strangely when they're near me, so I've kind of avoided them lately. And the way they look at me is just scary! I don't know what's up with them or what to do about it.'

Hearing this, Nico started to laugh out loud. She started to feel stupid, asking worthless questions randomly. Fortunately, the boy managed to stop laughing, and put a hand around her to cheer her up.

'Jennifer, do you know what 'love' means?'

'Um...no, nobody has ever told me.'

'Well then, do you know what 'like' is?'

'Well of course I know that! I hope you don't think I'm stupid!'

'No, no, nothing like that. What I'm trying to explain is that 'love' is a very powerful word for 'like', much more powerful.'

'Ok, I learnt a new word, now what's your point?'

'I might be wrong, but I think that my brother and Peter might feel something in between 'like' and 'love' when thinking of you,' he said with a wink. On the other side, Jennifer was simply stunned.

'So, what am I supposed to do now?'

'I don't know, I've never been in your place before.' He took a small break, thinking, 'Jennifer, do you like either of them in particular? I hope it's not too much to ask.'

'Well, they've both been very caring and kind...maybe even over the limits, but still, no. No, I don't like either of them in particular. They're both my best friends, and I don't want that to change,' she said with a gulp at the end, almost letting out those tears hiding in her eyes.

Nico stood up without warning, and then helped Jennifer up. It wasn't difficult to sense the girl's confusion and need to be alone, so he said:

'I think you should go and think about it, and clear things up with them tomorrow,' he said with a smile.

And so she did. They parted ways; Jennifer going directly to her room with a bitter taste in her mouth, and Nico to who knows where, each minding his, or her own business.

8

Assaulted

Ring! Rrrrrrriiiiiiiinnnnngggg!!!! Ring ring ring!! Ring...

Early in the morning, Jennifer's alarm clock was going mad. Still, she wouldn't budge, not bothering to stop it, so the ringing went on for another minute.

However, the ringing was so loud, you could hear it from the corridor, and when people started banging at the door, Jennifer finally woke up and realised what was with the unbearable noise.

When she stopped her alarm clock, the banging stopped as well, and everything seemed peaceful for a moment, but then the banging resumed, even louder than before.

'Come out!' she could hear someone shouting.

'Open the door! It's dangerous to stay inside!' someone else screamed.

What's going on? thought the girl, asking herself this same question over and over again.

The banging wouldn't stop, and neither did the shouting, so she quickly got dressed, and opened the door.

Whoever was there, grabbed her by the wrist and pulled her closer. Before she knew it, she was running along the corridor, trying to catch up with the mysterious person who had a hold on her. It didn't seem like someone she knew, but she hadn't had the time to check the man's face.

Something was clearly wrong, and soon she would find out what. Why is it dangerous to be inside? Wasn't inside supposed to be the safe place?

As she gave attention to those thoughts, she heard another person who was running along say:

'There is no safe place, we have to run!'

There were four men, including the one who had hold of her wrist, but she didn't bother to give attention to these things; she had to run, although she had no idea why.

'Let go of my wrist, I can run much better,' she said.

The man nodded and let go, and the five of them ran much quicker. Jennifer was somewhere in between them all: two men in front, two men in the back, and she was in the middle.

She was either trapped, or safe. *I hope that it's safe,* she thought.

'Where are we going?' she managed to ask between breaths. She waited for an answer. Eventually, one of the men from the rear said:

'We have to get to the colonel.' He made a pause to regulate his breathing, and resumed. 'He'll tell us each of our roles today...'

'Roles?' Jennifer cut him off.

'Yes, roles,' answered another. 'Like "go there and do that", "stay here and do this" and so on.'

The girl was still confused, but the man who previously had hold of her wrist seemed to sense her confusion, because he quickly added, 'As we speak, we are being attacked by the aliens, so we'd better hurry up before it's too late.'

There was no need for more words, because everything was now crystal clear for Jennifer; they were under attack, and had to prepare their defences and drive off the trespassers as quickly as possible.

***

'Peter, Mark, I have some special assignments for you two. Peter, you are to check the northern wing of the academy, and report to me immediately the situation there. There are already a couple of soldiers guarding that area, but I need to know whether we should strengthen our force on that side. After you report in, do the same with the eastern wing.'

Peter nodded and left without a word, running at full speed. He had no right to argue with the colonel, especially in such a critical situation as this, when every second mattered.

Quickly taking a pause to breathe, the colonel continued, addressing Mark this time:

'You are to accompany Jennifer all around the academy,

both inside and outside. I'm sure you have heard about our H4Ks, the hologram devices. You and Jennifer will place them all over the place, until there are none left. If we cannot outfight them, we've got to at least outsmart them.'

'Yes, sir. But where is Jennifer?' Mark asked, afraid that asking something now was wrong. However, the colonel didn't mind the possible disrespect and answered:

'She is bound to arrive any second now. She is being escorted, so when she gets here, get on with your mission. I'll let you explain to her what you've got to do. One more thing though. When you place those H4Ks, make sure not to be seen by any outsiders.'

'Yes, sir,' he said once more. He paced around the room, waiting for Jennifer to arrive.

He needn't wait long, because in less than a minute he could already see her and some other men running towards the room where the colonel gave orders.

Before she or the other men had time to reach the colonel, Mark grabbed the girl's hand and took her in the opposite direction.

'What's happening?' she demanded. 'Why is everyone pulling me by the hand today?'

'We've got to get moving and complete our assignment. I'll explain on the way.'

'*Our* assignment? You mean I'll be working with you on this one?' It wasn't obvious whether she was delighted, mad or frightened.

As Jennifer and Mark were leaving the room, the girl quickly glanced at the colonel who nodded. She was ready to listen to Mark. They both started running at full speed.

Finally, Mark answered her:

'Yes, we'll be working together on this one,' he said, putting the accent on 'together', and then he explained what they had to do.

'What about Peter?' she asked. 'What does he have to do?'

Mark rolled his eyes when hearing Peter's name, but Jennifer missed it.

'He has to scout the northern and eastern wings of the academy. Boring, right?'

'Might be, but at least he's not in as much danger as the majority of us.'

Mark stayed quiet to let the conversation die out. Fortunately for him, it worked.

The two of them were still running, reaching the lab in record time, feeling more exhausted than ever. The moment they got there, they spotted the H4Ks, which were in a bag, grabbed it and left the lab without wasting a single second.

'Wasn't my device the prototype?' the girl asked Mark.

'I think it was,' he answered while running.

'They must be working really hard if they were able to make so many in such a short amount of time.'

'Um-huh,' he agreed, and they focused again on the way they went. 'Go left, Jen. We'll start outdoors and make our way back inside.'

'I just hope we won't run out of them too soon,' she said, with a worried look on her face.

Soon afterwards, they reached the first place where they were supposed to place the H4Ks: the Inner Walls, which were surrounding the academy. In total, there were three layers of walls, each larger than another, forming circles which protected the Warband Academy.

The fighting was currently between the Outer and Middle Walls, but their forces would soon have to retreat to the Inner Walls which is where they were. They had to move quickly.

They hid behind some bushes while they made sure there was nobody spying on them, and placed a couple of holograms down, activating them. When they were done, it looked like an army of soldiers was guarding that area, even though they were no more than some projected images.

The plan was to scare off the alien invaders by making them think that the human forces were much more numerous than the alien forces. This will hopefully make them retreat quickly.

The moment they finished with that area, they moved on to the next, again hiding behind bushes while checking that the path was clear. The fighting hadn't reached them yet.

In less than a minute they were done with the second area, and could hear the fighting getting closer to them by the second. They had to get out of there quickly before any of the trespassers saw them.

Unfortunately, it was too late. Mark realised it when he looked up and saw an alien spaceship throwing explosives right at them.

'Watch out!' Mark shouted at the top of his voice so he could warn Jennifer. Still, as loud as he said it, she didn't hear him because of all the gun shots and explosions.

He had to save her before it was too late, so he ran at her, pushing her into the bushes, and falling over her in the process.

The bushes were scratching their skin, but they had to wait until the explosions stopped. It was too dangerous.

In only a matter of seconds, the explosives hit the ground, forming craters where they fell, causing a small explosion all around them. The explosion threw pieces of rock and mud all over.

Soon, it was all over. The explosions died out, and the two of them could finally get back on their feet.

Jennifer only had a couple of scratches from the bushes because Mark stayed between her and the explosions. He became a human shield for Jennifer. Mark took off the remains of his ripped shirt. His back was all muddy and full of bruises from the rocks that jumped when the explosions started.

'Ach!' he shouted when he got up. 'My back hurts like crazy!' *I don't regret anything though,* he thought. *Seeing Jen safe and sound is all I need.*

Without a word, the girl helped him stay upright, and supported him all the way inside, until he could finally rest for a moment. He thanked her, but she remained silent and turned around, looking the other way. Finally, she whispered:

'Thanks for saving me. I'm really sorry for what happened to you, I wish I could prevent it...'

'Jen, don't worry about me, I'm fine...ow!' he tried to say before the pain in his back returned stronger than before. 'It wasn't your fault. I'm just glad you're safe.' He smiled, but she still had her back to him, so she didn't see his kind and caring smile.

'Mark, I appreciate all you're doing, I really do... but I think you're overdoing it. Both you and Peter. I...um...' she said looking down and playing with her fingers. 'I know about you two...you care too much...far too much. Don't take me wrong, but I don't want anything to change,' she said. Jennifer ran off without even looking at him, which was somehow fortunate, because if she did, she would have seen him letting out a tear, and then another.

Everything was messed up. The H4Ks which weren't placed were destroyed with the explosion, and to make matters worse, Mark was hurt both on the outside and on the inside. Still, he kept thinking, *I still don't regret anything.*

9

Drama at the Academy

'What did she say?!'

'She said it like this: I know about you two...you care too much...far too much. Don't take me wrong, but I don't want anything to change.'

'The "you two" part is referring to us?'

'Of course! She even said it, you dumbo!'

'Ehm! I wasn't there when she said it, I was completing my assignment, without failing miserably and getting hundreds of high-tech devices destroyed for nothing,' said Peter, who was obviously in the mood to start an argument with Mark.

'So that's what you think happened? Don't you think that if I could save the H4Ks from being destroyed, I would?'

'I don't know, would you?' Peter said with a casual tone.

'Of course I would! But a human life is more important than some small devices, isn't that so?'

'When you put it like that...'

'Thank you!' said Mark sarcastically, rolling his eyes.

'But,' resumed Peter, 'If you had to choose between some devices and a random soldier you might not even know, which one would you save?'

Now Mark was speechless. He would've said a soldier because that was the right answer to Peter's tricky question, but he would have been lying; Jen's life valued much more than some devices, while a random soldier was just a random soldier. Mark decided to stay silent for a minute, and then tried to change the subject.

'I'm going to get some more training in before going to sleep,' he said with a frown, turning his back to Peter and walking away.

While Mark put some distance between them, he heard Peter shout from behind, 'I knew it! I just knew it!' Mark turned back around, ready to get to the bottom of whatever Peter 'knew'.

'What did you say?' he asked silently.

'I knew it! You love her, don't you?'

'You say it as if it's wrong, and as if you didn't yourself.'

'How would you know?'

'Because it's obvious how you try like a fool to make her see you?'

'Well, maybe I do,' he admitted, getting closer and closer to Mark. Soon they were pushing foreheads, like goats, intently looking each other in the eye. 'At least I do more than you!' he shouted.

'Prove it! Give me one thing you did for her to show that

you love her!'

'I, uh...I tried to make sure she wouldn't get hurt in fights!'

'As in letting her win? You know very well she hates that. It makes her feel weak and in need of protection; it's the worst thing you could do to her!' Mark shouted, pushing Peter a metre away, and slowly turning around to leave while whispering in between clenched teeth: 'but of course, you couldn't have known that. You're never paying attention to what she wants, needs or already has. Just the proof to show how much you care...' he ended sarcastically, and so silent Peter might have not even heard.

For another minute, Peter was left unable to move, shocked. Only afterwards he went the opposite way towards his room, while Mark went, as he earlier said, to get some more training in before sleep.

***

The training grounds were nearly empty because everyone preferred to enjoy life so long as they still had it, for the war could take it from their grasp at any time. However, Mark wasn't in the mood for such pleasures. His mind was crippled by only two things; war and Jennifer.

This evening, they were about to get mixed up.

Jennifer was lying on her back, trying to control her breathing before starting anew with training her swordsmanship. When he saw her, Mark stood hidden behind a corner and watched. She was training on a dummy, hitting it with all her power, and falling back when it wouldn't budge.

She ended up screaming at thin air, which made her look like a psychopath. In Mark's eyes, it was just a little thing which could put a smile on his face.

As much as Jennifer got annoyed with the practice dummy, she wouldn't give up. Unfortunately, she was starting to do worse as time passed, so Mark decided to get out of his hiding place, and moved closer to the girl in silence. As Jennifer had her back to him, she only found out of his imminent presence when he gently took hold of her arms, guiding them into a dance of swordsmanship.

The poor girl was paralysed. She really thought there was nobody watching her, and much less someone who would get hold of her and be able to control her moves. Some other person probably would've gotten a slap round the face, or much, much worse, but Mark didn't.

And so, they went on dancing with the dummy and the sword for a minute, until Jennifer froze completely, still shocked. She broke from his gentle grasp, and faced him. Her mouth was open, but no words would come out, so she gulped and tried again, but still, to no avail.

They stared at each other for another minute, until Mark broke the ice.

'I didn't know you were here,' to which Jennifer replied, 'I didn't know you were here either,' but with a rough voice, trying not to break out in tears. The sight of Mark just made her sad for the moment, or at least confused. She felt more confused than ever. She didn't know what to say or how to react, so she just stood there, petrified.

After a minute of silence, Mark started talking again. 'I

know you probably hate me, and I respect that. I don't want to try to change your mind, but if you want to talk about it, about anything, that's great. If you don't...it's okay...'

'No,' she said quickly. 'I mean...I don't know...' She threw herself on the floor because she needed something to support her. Mark placed himself in front of her, a very small distance away, yet leaning forward. Once she noticed, Jennifer leaned backwards as she was watching his eyes begging her to stay as close as possible.

After a while of looking at each other in an awkward silence, Mark suddenly changed the topic they've been trying to talk about for so long.

'Hey Jen, do you want some help with training?'

'I'm fine, thanks,' she said, looking away from him.

'If you say so...but I'm not so sure about that shouting, unless it's a new move, meant to scare the hell out of an opponent. Then I bet it's going to be the most brilliant move!' he said smiling, trying to cheer her up.

'You...you saw that? But that was like an hour ago...how long have you been watching?' the girl said, her face now red from fury, but feeling even more awkward than before.

'Um...maybe a couple of minutes before that? I'm not sure. I remember you just finished a break when I started spying... uh, I mean checking on you.'

'Oh, good. I suppose.'

'Back to my question. Do you want some help with training?' he said, feeling most anxious about it. The girl looked down, but smiled this time, and said with a shrug 'Sure, why not?'

'Ok, how about you first show me the shout move, eh?' he asked smiling.

'I'm not going to show you that!' she frowned, but he continued to mock her.

'Why not? Afraid you might just give me a fright?'

'Maybe.'

'I dare you! Scare me!' he said almost jumping with excitement.

'I told you I'm not going to do it,' she said calmly. 'So begging me will not get you anywhere.'

'Begging won't get me anywhere you say? Fine, no more training for you. Good night.'

'Great, I didn't want any more training anyway!' she shouted at him as he turned back, sighing too much and keeping his head down.

Sigh...he's a horrible actor, she thought. 'Fine,' she murmured.

'Is that a yes? I knew you would give in!' he said as he turned around to face her, with one of his childish and cute smiles.

'But just once.'

'We'll see about that,' he winked.

'I hate you so much!' she shouted in between clenched teeth, yet there was an obvious smile on her face, trying to stay hidden from sight.

***

'Good morning!' someone shouted, but got no answer. 'Ehm, I said *good morning!* Still no answer. 'Just get up already, kids!'

whoever said that, pushed Mark and Jennifer off their little 'bed' in the training hall.

They woke up simultaneously, and with a great fright too. It took them a while to realise it, but they had both fallen asleep while training the past evening, and now, after a few hours of sleep, Blockhead woke them up.

Sleepy and a little confused, the two kids rose to their feet, looking scared at their ruthless trainer, who just looked at them. Blockhead was shocked to find anyone in the training hall before himself, much less someone *sleeping* in the training hall...especially a boy and a girl.

'I know it's no written rule, but the training hall is no place for dates, kids,' he said, raising an eyebrow at them.

'*Date?!*' they both said in unison, looking at each other wide-eyed. 'Him? Me? No way!' said Jennifer, and so did Mark, just using 'her' instead. Still, they were both blushing, and trying not to make eye contact with each other.

'Well then what's your excuse for sleeping in the training hall?' Blockhead asked, frowning and crossing his arms.

'We had some extra training last evening, sir,' said Mark.

'Yes, sir. Mark helped me a bit with my swordsmanship and I helped him with flexibility and speed exercises. I think we make a great team, sir,' added Jennifer. Upon hearing those kind words, Mark just couldn't help but smile.

'So you say. Anyway, I hope you don't expect that that 'extra training' helped you get rid of your current, and not to forget obligatory training.'

'No, of course not, sir.'

'Very well, I shall keep a close eye on you two today,' he

said, turning around, about to mind his own business when he realised the training hall was empty except for themselves. It was barely 5 a.m. Nobody woke up that early, much less come to the training hall. This left the three of them alone for another two hours. Another couple of hours with Blockhead. The poor kids were going to be tortured by the time anyone else arrived.

The two of them gulped when they realised what was going to happen. 'How are we going to survive so long alone with... *him?*' quietly asked Jennifer.

'No clue, but I hope we'll make it through somehow.'

Blockhead still had his back to them, and addressed them without bothering to turn around. 'Since you, Mark, say that you helped her with her swordsmanship, and you, Jennifer, say that you helped him with some flexibility and speed exercises, how about we test what each of you learned, eh? Nothing better to do anyway, right?'

'Right...' they said in unison.

Jennifer lowered her head, already feeling defeated. How could she withstand that much time with Blockhead?! When he noticed her reaction, Mark put a hand on her closest shoulder, and whispered in her ear 'you'll be fine,' which, of course, she didn't believe. Also, in his mind, Mark thought *I wish I'll be fine myself...*

10

Return of the Vengeful One

Another day in hell...I can't wait for the morning training to be over already!

As usual, Peter was far from eager to go training. Little did it matter that he was one of the best trainees. When it came to brawling anyway. Peter and swordfights were like the Sun and the Moon, never going to be able to be together.

Annoyed and tired, he forced himself to get to the training hall. Anything was better than having Blockhead annoyed with you. Some say that he had taken lessons on torture, because he was so good at finding the worst of punishments that it made everyone obey to any foolish command of his. Fortunately, he wasn't *that* absent-minded.

Finally, Peter reached the training hall, and was surprised to see he was one of the first to arrive. There were a few other trainees, but he did notice three specific people; Mark, Jennifer and Zack. Zack was shooting evil looks at his precious little 'Jenny', yet not daring to approach her. Still, Peter was more surprised of the fact that his two friends were wide awake, and sweating already. It was roughly 6:30 in the morning. When could they have had the time to start *sweating*?!

He couldn't just stay curious, so he went over and without even greeting them, he went directly to the point. Between breaths, the two awkwardly told him what had transpired, but they kept the details to themselves. Peter knew they were hiding an important part of their story as his face showed doubt, but he didn't ask any more questions.

'Jenny, Zack keeps looking at you. What's wrong with him?'

'Oh. Him again... Well, he's just jealous I suppose. Remember I defeated him once? Since then he's been like this. I'm surprised you noticed just now.'

'Well, I did notice a while ago, but I thought it was nothing of importance.'

'Do you guys think there's any way to make him forget about it all? After all, it's nothing much. He's been winning and losing fights every day. Just like everyone else,' added Mark.

'Yea, but he was never defeated by a girl before. He's still not over it apparently.' thoughtfully said Jennifer.

'Well then, I only see one solution to this problem,' started Peter. 'You have to let him defeat you.'

'I hate to admit it, but he might right, Jen,' added Mark with a low voice.

'I don't like the idea. Still let's suppose I do let him win. How on Earth am I going to do that without ending up in hospital again?'

'How about just dodging, parrying, blocking all his attacks, and then pretend you can't go on any longer,' suggested Mark.

'Like that's gonna fool him. He just won't stop until he *does* find a way to obviously hurt me more than I apparently hurt him...I suppose I have no option...'

'Jen, are you sure about it? I don't want you getting hurt just to make him happy,' worriedly said Mark.

'Mark, you do realise you just interrupted me, right?'

'Oh, sorry.'

'So, I was saying that I have no option but talk to him about it. We've got to clear things up somehow...'

After a couple of seconds of waiting for an approval from the two boys, the girl refused to continue waiting and started walking towards Zack, but Peter's hand on her shoulder stopped her.

'Jenny, are you sure about this? He's not the sort you can just talk some sense into, you know.'

'Do you have a better idea?'

'No...'

'Then yes. I'm sure,' she said. 'Oh, and one more thing... whatever happens, please don't interfere. It's my problem, not yours, and I don't want you two involved.'

She left to talk with Zack. The two boys stayed behind, watching from a distance. They watched Jennifer and Zack start to talk but they couldn't hear what was being said.

'Hey, Zack!'

'Jennifer? What is it you want?' he asked with an obviously bored voice.

'I just wanted to talk...you know, about our last fight.'

'You were just lucky. Don't expect to defeat me next time,' he said with a mischievous grin.

'So...we're good?' she asked, hopeful for a positive answer, yet it never came. After a few seconds, he shouted:

'No!' He launched himself at Jennifer, grabbing her loose hair, doing anything he could to make her suffer. It was his payback.

As shocked as Jennifer was, she had expected something like this to happen so she was prepared. As quickly as possible, she grabbed his hands to keep them from pulling her hair. Making sure he didn't fall back, Jennifer raised her knee and hit Zack in the stomach. This was meant to stun him for a short while, but it was nothing serious. Still, as the girl expected, he let go of her hair, so she managed to take a few steps back until he regained his breath. By now, more people started coming in the training hall, and all of them gathered, of course, around them. Even Blockhead was watching curiously, yet not daring to stop them; he was enjoying the view far too much.

*I knew I'd end up fighting him...I must let him win somehow, so all this will finally end. But how? I still value my life...and I'm sick of staring at the hospital ceiling...*she thought.

While she was trying to figure out a way to let him win without getting herself killed, Zack had already regained his breath, and was running towards her. He was aiming for the head, so she leaned back to avoid the hit. Of course, the boy anticipated that, and was prepared to take advantage of it. Jennifer watched Zack's hand touch her nose as she leaned back. He broke her equilibrium and made her fall on her back with a powerful thud.

What could she do now? She was on the floor, and he had the advantage. The girl felt cornered, and felt her heart beat as fast as the speed of light. She knew the boy would hit her, aiming for the face as usual. There was no time to fully dodge his attack, but she did manage to turn her head to her left side. He managed to hit her right cheekbone. The pain was unbearable, but she wouldn't let this be the end. If he wanted a fight, he might as well have a very good one.

Still, she wouldn't react just yet. She pretended to close her eyes as if knocked out, but between her eyelashes she could see all she needed; Zack thought he had already won, so he backed away a couple of steps, tasting the victory. There were many gasps from the public. This diversion gave her the time and space to get back up on her feet, and see his surprised, yet still confident look on his face.

Once upright, Jennifer's first instinct was to put her hand to her face. When she moved her hand away, she saw that her hand was covered in fresh blood. The pain was growing until that half of her face felt numb. She managed to dodge a few more attacks, but her right leg was badly bruised, and an older cut on her left arm was now torn back open and bleeding.

Soon, Jennifer lost so much blood that she suddenly fell to the floor without Zack having to hit her. At first, the boy wasn't sure whether she was faking it again, so he only realised his victory after checking she was unconscious for real.

For Zack, this victory was sweet. Seeing Jennifer unconscious on the floor made him feel like nothing better could happen. For Mark and Peter, the sight of seeing their best friend lying unconscious was grievous, simply horrible. Without a second thought, they ran to her, picked her up and went straight for the emergency hall.

On their way, Blockhead stopped them for a few moments. 'After you deal with her, and do it quick too, return back here. I've got some tasks for you,' he said, but stopped and started talking again, all of a sudden. 'No, actually. Mark, you have shown me enough for today. You're free for the rest of the day. Peter, you shall return here, and I'll have you brawl Zack. Someone needs to get payback for Jennifer, and I think you're fit for the job,' he said, with a *wink*!

A little suspicious, the two boys nodded and left without a word in a great hurry. They didn't talk on the way, but it was obvious what they were thinking, especially what Peter was thinking. *Lucky him. He gets almost a whole day off, and can even stay and take care of Jenny...humph!* When they finally laid her down on a bed, Mark took a seat on a small chair he found in the ward. 'Make sure she'll be fine,' Peter said then he left in a hurry to get payback.

There was no way Zack was getting away with that! Peter refused to let him win, no matter the price.

As expected, Peter won, but their fight certainly was a deadly one. The two were at each other's throats, and only stopped when Blockhead demanded they end right that instant.

The good news was that Zack would leave Jennifer alone from now on, though he still couldn't stand her.

11

Scars are Forever

'W-what happened?' She coughed, spitting blood all over the place.

'Jen, are you alright?'

'Look at me, am I?'

He didn't answer. Instead, Mark gave her half a hug, as she was laying in bed, unable to move.

'So what happened?' she insisted, so Mark told her.

'You were brawling Zack...and I don't know how you managed to let him hit you so often, but when he hit you, he must've opened some of your older cuts, because you were bleeding from several spots. The hit on your cheekbone was the worst though...you lost a lot of blood because of it, and ended up fainting. Peter and I brought you here as quickly as we could.'

He suddenly stopped talking because he found it way too

hard to say anything more. His throat was burning, and tears were already leaving his eyes. 'I was so scared...' he managed to add, 'that you wouldn't make it...'

'Shh...' she begged. 'I'm fine, but I need sleep. So shh...' she managed to whisper. Her eyes were still closed, but she could feel him coming nearer, until he gently kissed her forehead. 'Don't leave me alone...please.'

'I'd never do that,' he promised, but the girl couldn't hear him anymore because she had already fallen back asleep.

***

While sitting on the chair next to Jennifer's bed, waiting for nothing in particular, Mark fell asleep. Soon afterwards, the girl opened her eyes yawning, but not moving any more than that. The pain was horrible. All she could do was watch the ceiling...the ceiling she got so bored of.

I think I end up in hospital the most! she thought, upset.

While there, not being able to do anything, she wished for something, anything to happen. Eventually, it did. After an hour of waiting and watching Mark sleeping on the chair next to her, someone came in, nearly as silent as a rabbit.

At first, she heard the door crack open, letting out a soft creak, and then closing. The sounds were faint though, but as there was no other noise to hear, these faint sounds were almost clear. After the door closed, Jennifer heard soft steps approaching, becoming louder as they got nearer. She didn't recognise the pattern...it was a strange one, so she got scared. The steps went like one-two-two, one-two-two, as if the person walking was taking half a step at a time with one of his feet. This pattern was foreign, so Jennifer started to freak out.

Wake up, Mark, wake up! But he didn't wake up. It didn't matter what was going to happen, she was on her own. She tried to stay silent, and hoped the mysterious person would leave, but he seemed to know exactly where to go. Directly towards her.

Finally, the intruder was right in front of her, but the darkness in the room camouflaged his figure. All she could see was that he was very tall and slim, maybe a bit too slim. *Have I ever seen someone looking like this before? I greatly doubt it. So, who in the world is this guy?!* She was completely freaked out.

A minute passed, and the figure didn't move. Before anything happened, she noticed that the intruder was wearing a long black hooded robe, which hid every single body part. *Please tell me this is a dream,* she begged in her mind. Unfortunately, this strange event was real, and she'd never forget it.

Soon, she heard some foreign voice in her mind...most probably the intruder's. It sounded very strange, and high pitched, just as if it was heard though a device, but also making quick pauses in between every single word, and it said: *I see you are in great pain.*

How could she answer? She could barely move her eyes around, much less move her lips to talk, and she was also too freaked out to say a thing. Quickly, the figure continued: *You do not have to answer. There is no need. I will help. But you will come with me.*

Jennifer's mind flooded with questions when hearing those

telepathic words, 'Why? How? What's going to happen?' Poor Jennifer was traumatised, but she couldn't do anything about it.

Jennifer's eyes were wide open in shock. After a few moments, she closed them and gave in. In her condition, there was nothing she could do about it.

A couple of minutes later she opened them again, with the hope that it was just a nightmare, but instead she found herself in a completely different environment. It took her a while to process the fact that she had just been kidnapped by the humans' war enemy, the aliens.

Who knows why they brought her there, wherever 'there' was, and what they had in mind…?

***

After a long while of sleeping, Jennifer's eyes opened to see the 24-hour clock in her room telling her it was midnight. For a moment, she thought it didn't mean anything, but then she realised that she hadn't fallen asleep in her room… wasn't she somewhere else? She couldn't remember where, so she stood up and walked in circles around the room, thinking.

Something told her that that little piece of information was more important than it appeared. Also, she had the feeling something was wrong. Wasn't she severely injured after her brawl with Zack? How could she move so freely and without any pain at all? What had transpired?

As she went on asking herself such questions, she noticed something moving in the far corner of the room, where the light found it hard to reach. Even though she was tired, she was certain that it wasn't her imagination playing tricks on her. Slowly, she approached the place, guard up.

By the time she got there, Jennifer discovered that nothing was there. She caught, in the corner of her eye, a glimpse of movement on the ceiling. It was right above her, moving behind, so she quickly turned around to see where it went, whatever it was.

She lost sight of it, and reminded herself that she was tired and paranoid. This gave her enough reason to go back to sleep, with the intention of forgetting about whatever she thought she had just seen.

With slow movements, she neared her bed and sat down. Before she would lay down, she looked one last time around the room, still wondering how she got there. While doing so, she noticed that the top of her alarm clock was now blue, and it seemed larger. She remembered it being plain gray, and much smaller. Simply out of curiosity, she reached for it, trying to put her fingertips on the blue part.

Even in the dim light, she saw how the blue part moved in a flash of a second, stopping right next to the clock. The girl retreated her hand, shocked by what she had just seen, but had no idea that what would follow will be even more incredible.

The blue moving thing seemed to expand, becoming taller, as big as thirty centimetres. Out of nowhere, appeared two large black eyes somewhere at the top, where its head apparently was. When two thin feet and two yet thinner hands appeared, the blue thing started to look like a miniature human being, more or less.

While this process took place, Jennifer was watching,

feeling both terrified and amazed at every detail, asking herself more and more questions. What could it be? Maybe it was the answer to some of her previous questions. Either way, it was bound to bring even more unanswered questions.

Why was that thing in her room? What purpose did it serve? Could it be an alien? She was pretty sure it was indeed an alien, but it seemed so very different from whatever she had hitherto imagined that she found it hard to accept the idea of it being an alien. Another of her questions, probably the most critical of all: did it come in peace, or otherwise, more unpleasant terms? It looked harmless, but she very well knew that things are never what they seem to be. This gave her enough reason to become scared.

Still, all she could do in her shocked state was watch, and wait.

12

Friends or Foes?

Jennifer couldn't decide what to do, so she simply stayed there unblinking, cautiously watching the little blue creature.

She was more than certain it was an alien, and aliens were their enemies, so why wouldn't she attack or call for help? It's not like she couldn't, yet she didn't. What could've been stopping her?

It was most probably her own conscience. Her instincts told her that whoever...or whatever the creature was, it meant no harm.

A few minutes probably passed, but the girl and the blue creature didn't move the slightest bit. It was just as if time had frozen them in place. In the meantime, the girl was crippled by strange feelings...not thoughts this time, but just feelings. It was just as if she was meant to meet that creature, and that a hidden goal of hers had been accomplished without her even knowing of its existence. She felt *whole*.

Soon, she finally heard some sounds which she thought were in another language, but she only realised it when familiar words showed up.

I am sorry, I forgot you are a humanoid and that you speak naught our language. My knowledge of humane language is poor, so my apologies if you understand naught of what I say.

The creature took a couple of seconds break, which gave Jennifer the liberty of letting a wide smile and murmured 'you're doing fine, go on.'

Thank you kindly. First, I ought to communicate my name. It is Blurreydal, but you may call me as you want. Now, my mission. I must communicate to you what happened...I believe you are confused. The girl nodded in agreement, after which Blurreydal went on. *You were hurt and close to death, so we took care of you. How you wonder...well, one of our scientists came to... fetch you from where you were. He teleported you on to one of our spaceships, where he made sure you would be fine. Then he brought you in this room which appears to be very personal to you.*

The girl's eyes were wide open and full of wonder. She thought she was dreaming, and this couldn't be reality. Either way, Blurreydal went on without minding her shocked expression.

My true quest? The first thing is done; I communicated to you the explanation of the possible confusion. Now? It is time to help and make things as they should be. Our very different races are opposing each other as you know, but this should not happen. Long ago, some of my kind have come in terms of peace, but your Men were ignorant and cast us out. I was sent to make sure this changes, and it will change somehow if us two work together.

You must understand that we only want your friendship. Also, your leaders must know this. They will not believe it, but they should somehow. We must make them understand. They have to 'open their eyes', like you, humanoids, say, and see that they are destroying themselves by fighting.

However, you must know that not all of your kind are against my kind, but you will find out who that is on your own. Also, remember you were not the first, and will not remain the last chosen for the task.

The small blue creature finally stopped talking, and left the girl feeling more shocked than ever. She wasn't sure what she was expected to do now. Why did the aliens pick her to help in all this? Is what Blurreydal says true? Can she trust him, her, it, whatever it was? What the little alien said seemed true enough and with good reason, so she eventually accepted the fact that it was trying to help.

'I have so many questions...' she whispered, the only noise in the room.

I will answer best I may. We must get to know each other if this is to work; become friends. I want you as a friend. I hope you do too. I shall tell you all you want to know of me, or my kind, and you will tell me of yours. I want to see what your life is like.

'See it? How?' and right then, the little blue creature made a sudden move, transforming itself into a wonderful blue bracelet on Jennifer's arm. All this sudden movement took her by surprise, so she grimaced as she watched with curiosity what was happening.

I can come with you anywhere if you want me to. Nobody will know. They can't hear me; I speak to you alone... Jenif?

'Actually, it's Jennifer, but you can call me Jenif if you want,' she said, smiling. 'Can I call you Blur?'

I love it, Jenif, my friend.

And so, the night went on quicker than expected. Jennifer and Blurreydal exchanged memories, feelings, even images just by thinking of them. The girl found out lots of interesting facts about aliens, including a bit of their history, although nothing related to the war. In exchange, the little alien found out some details about some of the Men's barbaric customs.

By the time Jennifer's alarm clock started ringing, the two of them were already having a wonderful time together. The ringing reminded Jennifer that it was time to go to training, she simply sighed.

Oh no, my friend Jenif is sad. What is it that is bothering you, Jenif?

'It's just the daily routine... I've got to have a quick breakfast and right after I must show up in the training hall... and if I'm late, Blockhead will surely find some way to punish me.'

Time to eat then. Quick, quick, quick!

The little creature's excitement made the girl smile for a brief second. She then got up from bed, put on her usual clothes which were getting worn out already, and rushed out of her room. While she was getting ready, Blurreydal turned into a blue, thin, barely noticeable necklace around her neck. When the girl caught glimpse of it in the mirror, she quickly said: 'Um, Blur? Do you mind staying as a bracelet? I think a necklace will be uncomfortable during training...' Before managing to finish her sentence, the little alien transformed itself into a sapphire bracelet on her left wrist.

Time for breakfast now. In record time, Jennifer had a portion of eggs and bacon from the academy cafeteria, and sprinted her way to the training hall, pushing to the side whoever stood in her way. She was going to be late!

When she entered the training hall, a pair of eyes was watching her furiously. 'You're ten seconds late, Jennifer. Tick tock, tick tock, every second counts, now get to work! Warm-up, and then we'll see what's next.'

The girl froze into place when she saw her trainer waiting for her, but was relieved to know that she wouldn't be punished for those ten seconds...yet.

Meanie! Who does he think he is to treat you like that!

'That's Blockhead...' she whispered, so that none other than Blurreydal could hear. Still, she seemed as if she was talking on her own, which would probably freak out whoever was nearby. A moment later she added a loud sigh, and spoke to herself, 'warm-up...yay...' Still, she wouldn't complain any more about it. At least the warm up was more peaceful than the rest of the training.

While she was doing her usual exercises, Blurreydal kept asking her who's this, who's that, why do you do this, and so on, to which the girl tried to answer as briefly as possible, and silently too, so as to not attract attention. Eventually, the questions stopped when someone neared her, telling her 'good morning' and smiling. The little alien was too curious to watch what happened to ask anything else.

'Oh, good morning, Peter.' She raised her head to look

at him when she noticed he had a black eye, so she instantly gasped. 'What happened?'

'What? Oh, the eye! Right...After you fought Zack and he won, Blockhead put me to fight him too. After a few minutes he fell down on the floor, powerless, but by then he managed to get me quite bad...but don't worry about me, I'll be fine. I'm just glad I managed to get revenge for you,' he said smiling. Meanwhile, Blurreydal was closely inspecting every detail; his nervous gestures, the slight shiver in his voice, and those sweet eyes...eyes with which he looked at the girl. Still, the little blue alien wouldn't say a word.

'Oh, that's great. Thanks, Peter. I should get back to my warm-up now...'

'Oh, sorry, I didn't mean to interrupt...I'll leave you to it,' he said, almost scared she would get mad at him for some reason. She gave him a quick smile as he turned around and then she continued with her exercises.

By the time she finished, she felt full of energy. She even did some gymnastics exercises, just to make sure she was in good shape. When the backflip turned out well for the first time in her life, she was more than certain she was ready for anything. What was curious though, she never even *thought* of doing a backflip before, much less do it without problems. Anyway, she wouldn't let such thoughts bother her. Right now she had to concentrate on training.

Blockhead noticed that she finished her warm-up, though he didn't see her spectacular backflip. He neared her with a notebook and a pen in his hands. He seemed to have quite a long 'to-do list' for that day. Looking at his notebook,

Blockhead told Jennifer 'the first thing today is to pick someone to practice your swordsmanship with, and ten minutes later come in the centre of the hall and duel. Second, do the same with brawling. Next will be a surprise. Now get moving!'

A surprise? It was most probably her punishment for being ten seconds late. She wasn't waiting for it eagerly, but she wouldn't let this thought keep her from her work. She was determined to be the best today!

What was the first thing? Sword fight? What is that all about? asked Blurreydal.

'You'll see,' whispered the girl. Now she had to find herself a practice partner with whom she would have to duel later. The first person who came to mind was, of course, Mark, since he was an excellent swordsman, and a fearless foe. Unfortunately, she didn't see him anywhere, so she had to improvise. While she was searching for someone, Blurreydal asked what she was doing, and if her wandering around was what sword fighting meant. Unfortunately for the little blue alien, Jennifer didn't answer. She was concentrating on something else entirely and didn't even hear the question.

Eventually, after a couple of minutes of searching, she saw someone she knew would be a worthy opponent, although she had never fought with him before. She had in mind some guy called Caliban. He was much taller than her, more muscular than his body would let show, with messy dark hair and curious olive eyes. *The perfect replacement opponent,* she thought.

Jennifer approached Caliban. It turned out that he was also looking for an opponent so he gladly agreed. After practising for ten minutes, making sure they didn't hurt each other, they went to the centre of the hall. Everyone was watching, ready for the duel to begin.

On the way, they had the liberty of a minute's chit-chat, which is when Caliban noticed Jennifer's bracelet and asked where she got it from. 'Um...the bracelet? I...I just found it in my room. Someone probably left me a mystery gift, I don't know.' He seemed doubtful, but still he just said 'fair enough' and left her in peace. Jennifer noticed he had a small, dark grey, almost black, tattoo on the right side of his neck in the shape of a sword, but she didn't say anything about it.

The duel began. At first, the girl focused on self-defence, so as to save energy. Her tactic was to leave her opponent exhausted, ready for one final blow. Everything went as planned, except the final blow. It seemed like the boy had some hidden reserves of energy left, and he managed to parry her hit without a problem. This was enough to turn the tables; now Jennifer was left exhausted. She didn't see this coming, so now she had to improvise. He had the advantage of strength, but that didn't prove a disadvantage for her; she knew how to use his own strength against him, so she did just that. In a couple of seconds, Caliban ended up having his sword slip from his hand, and it flew a few metres away. It was too far for him to reach in time, so he raised his hands in defeat and the duel ended. Surprisingly, none of them ended up hurt, only exhausted.

Everyone cheered and clapped, which made Jennifer smile. *So, this is a sword fight*, said Blurreydal. *We have this also, but we call it Paiyle Grumm. Paiyle is our word for 'sword'*, *and Grumm is everything related to a fight, for example a duel.* Jennifer was listening fascinated, but didn't dare answer because Caliban was right next to her.

'You put up a great fight, Jennifer. You're an excellent swordswoman. I feel honoured to be defeated by one with so much experience,' he said, trying to be kind. A moment later, after seeing her blush, he went on talking. 'I forgot to tell you… your bracelet is very nice. I especially like the deep blue colour. Is it made of sapphire?'

Why was he insisting so much on the bracelet? Jennifer tried to answer casually, although she probably didn't manage to. 'I think so. I don't really care what it's made from, I just like the looks of it,' she managed to say. All he added before saying goodbye was 'never judge a book by its cover,' along with a wink. As he turned around, the girl noticed again the grey tattoo on the right part of his neck, but the shape was different. Now it pictured a flag. Probably the white flag used to symbolise defeat. Still, the change was curious, which left the girl thoughtful for a while, until Blurreydal told her: *I feel your need to talk about it. We will talk about it when we get back. Back to your room.* The girl just nodded, without a sound.

Now she just had to focus on the rest of her training. She had to do the same with brawling; find someone to train with for ten minutes, and then go in the centre so that everyone would see them, and let the fight begin.

Time passed quickly this time. Jennifer wouldn't pick Peter to fight her, because she knew she didn't stand a chance, so she looked for someone else. Eventually Jennifer found a guy called Leonard to brawl with her. Everyone called him Leo because of his fluffy golden hair, black eyes and vampiric teeth which made him look like a lion in its human form. Fortunately for Jennifer, his build wasn't as sturdy as Peter's, and his strength was limited to about half of his, so this made the girl's victory much easier.

Now she had finished all that Blockhead had planned for her…but he mentioned a third thing too, didn't he? Jennifer remembered it was the surprise element. Proud, yet a little scared, she neared her trainer, who was still looking in his new notebook. He had watched her two victories and noted down a few things. When he noticed she was there, he looked at her and said:

'Ready for your surprise task?'

The girl gulped and with a faint voice, she said she was as ready as ever.

'Alright then, get Caliban and Leonard here and I'll explain to you three what you have to do,' he commanded. When Blockhead noticed the confused look on Jennifer's face, who was still standing there, unblinking, he added, 'NOW!' Finally, she moved without a word, doing as she was told.

The two boys were just as confused as her, but she finally managed to get them to come with her to Blockhead. Now instead of one confused person, there were three. What was next? Nine confused people?

13

The Surprise Element

The three *musketeers* were watching Blockhead with curious eyes, waiting for him to give them their surprise assignment for the day. Eventually, after quite some time, he started talking.

'So you're probably wondering what this surprise is all about, and what all of you have to do with it,' he paused, giving the three a moment to nod, after which he went on. 'Today you have the privilege of trying something new, and to test the newest set of weapons designed especially for this war.'

The kids' eyes were as wide as plums by now, that's how surprised they all were. With a slight taste of fear in his words, Leonard asked with a low voice:

'What weapons, sir?'

'They're plasma blasters. That should answer your question. Their official name is P1B. Of course, our scientists are ready to start working on better versions of it, but only after these ones are already tested. So how about you give it a try?'

Rhetorical question. That 'question' of his was more of an order rather than anything else. Still, Blockhead managed to say it suspiciously kindly.

Once the three of them nodded in agreement, their trainer waved a hand in the direction of a new area of the training hall. It was made especially for plasma blaster training. Feeling very excited, Jennifer, Caliban and Leonard went towards the new area, feeling honoured to be chosen for these tests.

These things are strange, but they don't affect my kind, said Blurreydal. In order to answer, Jennifer whispered: 'All the better, I can have some fun,' to which the little blue *bracelet* started giggling.

Excited to get started, Jennifer grabbed one of the three P1Bs and turned to face the target. It was a titanium wall with red and yellow circles marking the spots you're expected to shoot at. Of course, for protection, there is special gear they had to use; anti-sound headphones and double-powered sunglasses. Jennifer guessed that the weapons let out a deafening sound and blinding light, which made it very dangerous for the people around. No wonder this new part of the training hall was in a separate room.

Like I said, it will not affect us. We don't need to see if we don't want to - there are plenty of other senses we may use - and have nothing to hear because we mostly talk telepathically, said Blurreydal. *Also, the human boy from the Paiyle Grumm... Caliban? Yes, he is looking.*

Looking? Looking at what? Probably at the weapons.

Maybe he was just as amazed as Jennifer. When the girl turned her head slightly, she noticed in the corner of her eye that his face was showing no expression. None at all. And he was looking *at her.* No. He was *staring* at her. She quickly focused back on the weapon, pretending that she didn't notice him. Still, he wouldn't flinch.

After a couple of minutes of trying, in vain, to hit the target, Jennifer finally gave up. Those things were so big and heavy that she could barely hold them, much less use them! Eventually she put the weapon and special gear back to their places, and turned to find Caliban still looking in her direction.

'Aren't you trying?' she asked, politely.

'Huh? Oh sorry, I suppose I got lost in my thoughts. I will now.' *Aha, sure. Your thoughts about what?* Asked the girl in her mind, but the question never came out of her mouth.

'It's quite fun actually, but very hard. Don't forget to get the extra gear, the headphones and glasses.'

'I will, thanks,' he said without looking at her anymore, and leaving.

As she was watching him get further away from her, she noticed his tattoo again; this time it was a thin hollow circle with a spot in the centre. *Am I imagining things, or is that thing actually changing?* If it was, then it obviously represented a feeling or object he was thinking of. *The circle looks similar to the bull's eye on the targets...nothing to worry about,* she told herself.

Jennifer watched as Caliban and Leonard practised trying to manoeuvre the new weapon, before heading back to her room. Jennifer didn't realise it, but Blurreydal noticed that after the girl turned around, the boy from the Paiyle Grumm was behind them, stalking her. For some reason, the little blue alien didn't tell its friend, Jenif, about it. She only found out about Caliban when she went to open the door of her room.

'Caliban?' she asked, unsure. A moment later, he suddenly appeared from behind the corner. 'Were you following me?'

'Me? Uh, of course not! My room's just behind the corner...' he started out saying, but when Jennifer showed him the I-don't-believe-you look, he added along with a sigh: 'Fine, I did follow you, but that's because I need to talk to you.'

'Go on then,' she calmly said. 'You can tell me now.'

'Um...I'd rather not here...you know, even walls have ears.'

'Oh,' she murmured. She understood that he wanted to talk in private, so she invited him in her room for a little chat while listening to Blurreydal's constant giggling. 'Sorry, I've got no chairs here, but you can take a seat on the bed. Sorry for the mess.'

'Don't worry about it, my room's much worse,' he said smiling.

All of a sudden, when each of them had a seat on the bed, the wonderful blue bracelet on Jennifer's hand jumped off, behind her. Blurreydal transformed itself into the little blue human-like shape. At the same time, the dark tattoo on Caliban's neck did the same thing. The two little aliens laid down next to each other, watching the boy and the girl.

'Wha-' Jennifer managed to say with a gasp, as Caliban started laughing. 'You...it...what?!' she was obviously confused.

'I suppose this explains why I followed you.'

'And why you kept going on about my bracelet...'

'And why you kept staring at my tattoo.'

'You noticed? How is that possible?'

'Oh, I didn't. My pal here did and told me. His name is Smolther by the way.'

'My friend's name is Blurreydal, but I call him Blur...' she turned to look at the little alien and continued. 'You knew about this and didn't tell me?'

I said to you we were going to talk about it when we reach your room. And we talk now.

'Yea, but I was talking about the fact that he was following me...' she looked back at Caliban. 'Sorry, I was talking with Blur.'

'Don't worry about it, it's my fault actually. I asked Smotch to tell your little friend not to mention it,' he said smiling.

'Smotch? You're talking about Smolther, right?'

'Yea, sorry. And sorry again for not wanting you to know that I was following you.'

'Apologies accepted, but if you don't stop saying sorry right this instant, consider yourself kicked out of here,' she said, with half a smile. He opened his mouth to say that word again, but closed it and only nodded when he realised that he would've been kicked out. 'Anyway, I suppose you didn't come all the way here for nothing, so what is it you want to tell me exactly?'

'Well, about that, we have to talk about our little friends.' He turned to look at Blurreydal and Smolther for a second, and then looked back at Jennifer. 'I only met Smotch a week ago. I found myself lying in my bed when the last thing I remembered was trying to see behind the gates, and fell right when I was about to see behind...'

'You...you actually climbed up there? And fell from that

distance? I must be talking to a ghost then!'

'I thought I was a ghost too when I woke up, but Smotch was there to explain to me what happened. The aliens revived me and brought me back before anyone else noticed I was missing. They don't even remember I climbed there, although plenty saw me. So, what's your story?'

'I ended up in hospital after a brawl with Zack... he nearly killed me, and I was losing a dangerous amount of blood. That's when a dark silhouette showed up. The next thing I remember was that I was in my room, and met Blur. I also noticed that nobody brought up the subject that I was close to death, nor the brawl itself, so I assumed that I was unconscious for so long that everyone just forgot or something.'

'Interesting...and when did this happen? I mean, when did you meet Blur?'

'Last night, why?'

'Trying to see what I can find out. I'm thinking it could help us figure out some important details in this stupid war.'

'You have a point,' she said. While Caliban was thinking what all that meant, Jennifer asked: 'Do you think Mark will remember me being in hospital, even though nobody else will? Or will Zack remember he won the brawl?'

'Why would Mark remember that?'

'He was in the same room with me when the silhouette appeared...just asleep.'

'Well that makes things all the more complicated,' he said, frowning. 'You have to ask him, but in case he doesn't remember, just change the subject so he doesn't get suspicious. We've got plenty of problems as it is.' Jennifer only nodded.

Caliban continued to think on the matter, but Jennifer was too bothered by the fact that she might have to brawl Zack again and that Mark might've forgotten that he didn't let her down when she needed him the most. But she remembered. That mattered enough, right? At least she knew his intentions better than himself, which was strange, but made her feel like she had the upper hand. Still, she already felt how her eyes were sinking in tears, both of joy and fear, and she refused to let anyone see her.

'It's getting late. Is there anything else you want to tell me?' He raised an eyebrow before answering.

'I didn't say sorry, why are you kicking me out?' he laughed. 'Alright, I intruded your privacy for long enough. One last thing though, I've got a request. Can you come by at my room after training tomorrow? I'll tell you all I managed to figure out on the matter.' He stood up and looked around the room before heading for the door. 'And I promise I'll clean up my room so well that it will be at least as clean as yours,' he added, making the girl let out a big smile. Caliban went out the door, taking his little black 'tattoo' with him. This time it showed a question mark.

I forgot to ask him about that!

Do not worry, intervened Blurreydal. *You can tomorrow, I will remind you if you want.*

That would be wonderful, thanks. And then she broke out in tears, minding her own minor problems she still had to deal with.

14

Finding Out...

The following day, Jennifer went to training as usual, with Blurreydal at her hand.

Luckily, there was no Blockhead to scream at her; he was too busy screaming at others for once. All of her friends seemed to be present, even Nico and Mark. Like usual, those two were staying with Peter, trying to train together. Jennifer went next to them.

'Good morning, boys, how are you?' She got no answer. 'Ahem, I'm here too, what are you talking about?'

'Huh, what? Oh, sorry Jen, we weren't exactly paying attention to whatever is happening around,' Mark said awkwardly.

'Anyway, what were you three musketeers talking about?'

'Nothing!' Nico joined in. 'I mean...nothing of importance, really.'

'And what is this not-important-subject?' she asked once more, but the boys only stared at her, not willing to tell her. 'It's not about me, is it?'

'Oh, look at the time!' Peter shouted, looking at the back of his hand, which of course had no watch. 'We ought to get some training done before Blockhead takes notice of us!'

And with those words, the three boys all went in different directions, leaving just the girl standing in the same place, confused and abandoned. Eventually, she ran after Mark. She needed to talk with him privately anyway.

'Mark, wait up!' He paced quicker. 'I challenge you to a duel.' He turned around to look at her.

'Now that's an offer I can't refuse. Grab a sword then, swordsman lady,' he said with a smile.

We'll see how much you'll be smiling after I'm done with you, the girl thought.

You have a plan, Jenif? I will lend you mine power.

The duel was about to start. The two of them were face to face, waiting for the other to make the first move, but neither of them would.

'So, you say you weren't talking about me. I believe you then.'

'I never said that,' he whispered, looking at the floor for a moment, then back at the girl, already making the first move. The girl dodged easily, and then slashed at him herself, although she knew he would block her blow.

After some more exchanges of blows, their blades were crossed and trembling, but not moving out of place. The weaker one would end up on the ground, at the opponent's mercy.

'Ready to lose?' he asked.

'I would think not,' she answered, and with Blurreydal's force, she pushed harder. Before he knew it, he ended up on his back, with a sword to his throat.

'Well done, Jen, you won the duel. Now can I get the liberty of staying upright please?'

'This is not over yet. Tell me what you were talking about when I showed up.'

'It was nothing, really.' He gulped.

'Lies!' She let the tip of the sword sink a little in his neck until she saw a stream of blood flowing out of his body and onto his skin.

'Fine, I swear I'll tell you, just get this sword out of my neck before it kills me!' Jennifer did just that; she distanced her sword from his neck, but remained in position, just so he wouldn't slip away.

'You're very smart, Jen. Did I ever tell you? I hate to admit, but we really were talking about you...But nothing bad, I promise.'

'What about me?' She frowned.

'I...I just told them about how you disappeared from the hospital ward when I woke up. What was strange though was the fact that they didn't remember you got hurt so badly, and not even that I went to stay with you...'

The girl didn't say a word, but only watched him talking, tears flooding her eyes. Quickly she turned around and threw the sword to her side. She walked away without another word.

Still on the floor, Mark was stupefied, and above all, very confused. He tried to get up, but his feet were numb and his neck was bleeding a little. 'Jen! Jen, wait up!'

'Training's over. I'm done here.' And she ran away.

***

'What?! Please tell me you didn't do that!' Caliban shouted.

'Why would I lie? Anyway, I managed to get the exact piece of information you asked me to get, maybe even more. I don't see the problem here.'

'The problem is that he is bound to be suspecting something...I don't like it. It's going to get nasty.'

'I don't think there's anything we can do right now, is there?'

'Indeed, you have a point. I don't know how we're going to solve this problem, but this is something we'll have to deal with on another occasion.'

'So back to our current problems...what was it again?' she asked.

'We have to figure out as much as possible about our little friends, why they came here exactly, and how we're supposed to work together to stop this war.'

Jenif, Jenif! You wanted to ask about the tattoo. Remember?

'Oh, right,' she whispered, and then looked at Caliban again. 'I wanted to ask you about Smolther. I noticed he always stays as a tattoo on your neck, just like Blur turns into a bracelet for me.'

'What about it though?' he raised an eyebrow.

'Either I'm blind and imagining things, or he's always taking a different shape. I was only curious if it means anything.'

'Oh, that.' He stopped for a second and laughed, and then resumed talking. 'It's pretty simple actually. Since he's staying as a tattoo on my neck, he's close enough to my brain to make direct contact with it. He gets the data from the part where the feelings are all stacked up, and takes up the shape of something representative, depending on my current feelings and thoughts.'

'Wow, that's quite awesome!' She turned to Blurreydal. 'Blur, can you do that too? Or do you have different powers or something like that?'

No, silly Jenif. We each are different, unique, special. I can use jewel metamorphosis, and Smotch goes 2D, like you call it. He can't do what I can, or I what he can.

'Oh, that's OK. I was just curious.'

'So,' Caliban joined in. 'What's our next move?'

'Hmm...I believe you mentioned that I met Blur exactly a week after you met Smotch, right?'

'Indeed, but what about it?'

'I'm thinking that maybe a week after my encounter, someone else is going to join in the party. It's only a theory, I'm not hundred percent sure.'

'It is possible there might be a pattern. You might actually be right. But in this case, all we can do is wait. I hate waiting.'

'I don't see what else we could do for now other than keep an eye open for anything that could help us,' she said, disappointed.

'It seems like it, yes. Well, I guess we're done for now. Keep in touch. Feel free to come by anytime.'

'Thanks, bye!' she said, and went out the door. Jennifer

turned around one last time before closing it, and said, 'I like how you cleaned up by the way,' and she closed the door just as the boy let out a large smile.

15

An Unexpected Visitor

Hello Jenif. You woke early.

'What's the time, Blur?' she asked yawning.

Half past four. You have almost two hours until training, what will we do?

'Um...no idea. What do you think we could do?'

For a minute there was silence. Other than a soft humming coming from Blurreydal, nothing else could be heard. Jennifer was just watching anxiously as the little blue alien was probably thinking. After a while, he answered, *I analysed the surroundings. There are two other people awake.* The girl was delighted, but that feeling suddenly vanished when she found out they were Mark and Caliban.

'What an unfortunate coincidence! What am I to do then?' Blurreydal couldn't understand the girl's problem, so he just stood silent as she was talking to herself. 'I can't go over to Caliban's, I was there yesterday evening, he'd think I'm desperate or something. And Mark...things get kind of awkward when it comes to him, and also, how could I explain how I knew he'd be awake so early?' After a short pause, she continued, still talking to herself. 'On the other hand, I need to apologise for how I reacted yesterday...' Finally, she turned to Blurreydal, asking 'what do you think I should do, Blur?'

You are right, Jenif. If you will go to one, it should be Mark. He is your friend, he will understand. At the moment, the girl couldn't figure out what Blurreydal meant in the last sentence, but was sure it wasn't important and let the thought slip away.

'Alright then, let's go.'

Silently, the girl left her room with Blurreydal at her hand in bracelet form and walked towards the boy's room just as silently. Meanwhile, she didn't even share a single word with the little alien, and neither did the alien tell her anything. For ten minutes she walked, watching the empty Academy corridors. Eventually she reached his room, but stopped in front of the door, staring at it. She almost reached for it to knock, but stopped midway and retreated her hand.

What is wrong, Jenif?

'I can't do it,' she whispered. 'He's bound to think it strange that I'm here at this hour.' Blurreydal didn't answer. After a few moments of standing in front of the door frozen, she suddenly sidestepped and leaned against the wall right next to the door, slowly falling to the ground. She softly bumped her head to the wall and then sunk her forehead in her knees, and just stayed there, not moving a muscle. 'What's the time?' she asked Blurreydal a minute later.

'It's a quarter to five.' The voice wasn't the alien's. Whose could it be? The girl raised her head and noticed that Mark had come out to the corridor and was curiously watching her, just as if she were an alien herself. 'What are you doing here?' he asked as he laid himself next to her on the floor, always looking at her with the same curious eyes. Did they show pity too? Or was that fright? The girl couldn't tell.

'What are you doing up so early?' she asked back.

'I could ask you the same thing.'

The girl sighed. 'I just woke up early, don't ask me how that happened. As for why I'm here, I just wanted to apologise.'

'Apologise for what?'

After a few moments, she answered, starting by taking a deep breath. 'For yesterday, for what I did and how I acted. For the day I disappeared from the hospital ward. For that day on the battlefield, when we were supposed to work as a team and I just left like that. For when I just ran away from you and Peter and fooled you with that hologram. For everything.' Her voice started fading, and she could feel burning tears making their way to the surface. 'I apologise for acting like a child and being so stupid.'

The young boy didn't know what to say, so he just stood there with his head lowered remembering all those painful moments. Their hands were close, touching the floor, and the boy thought of taking her hand, but stopped right before touching it and took it back without a word. Instead, he watched her bracelet, and thought it felt alive somehow. However, he forgot the bracelet and looked at Jennifer just as she turned her head so he wouldn't see her face.

'Jen...You don't need to apologise to me. You're not stupid, you never were and never will be. You're just being yourself, and that's more than I could ever ask for.'

'Then I hate being myself,' she managed to whisper.

'Don't say that! You've got a wonderful personality, and I wouldn't change it for anything in the world.' Then he was silent, waiting for her to say something, anything. Eventually, that something came and took him by surprise.

'Tell me, how many times did you get hurt?'

'Not so many times...'

'I'm not talking about physical pain only.'

'Oh. Well... A couple of times...' *Maybe a bit more than that*, he thought.

'And how many times was it my fault?' she whispered, almost angry. He wouldn't answer that. 'Exactly,' she murmured.

'But I don't care.'

'What do you mean?'

'I don't care about how many times I get hurt. I care more about you than I do about myself, so as long as you're safe and sound I'll always be happy. I don't know what I would do if something happened to you...'

Hearing those words, the girl remembered the night when he fell asleep in her hospital ward while watching over her. He must've stayed there doing nothing but watching her for hours, and wouldn't leave even though he was so tired he managed to fall asleep on a chair! At the thought, she just couldn't hold those tears any longer and burst out crying in her palms. For Mark, watching her cry felt like he was squashed and breathless and could do nothing about it. Without thinking, he put his hands around her and held her in a tight hug as she lowered her head on his shoulder.

'I'm so weak,' she managed to let out, and cried, 'I'm so sorry!' After that, she couldn't say another word before she would calm down.

The boy didn't even try to stop her from crying. 'Let's get you inside before anyone else sees you like this,' he whispered in her ear as he raised her from the ground. Once inside, he put her on the bed, and he stood next to her the whole time. Eventually, after a few minutes of crying without pause, the girl fell asleep. Of course, the boy would never take his eyes off her, making sure nothing happened to her, even though it seemed improbable there at that hour.

Time passed, and his alarm rang at six, but he closed it almost instantly so it wouldn't wake up Jennifer. She needed that sleep. However, if he didn't wake her up, they'd be late for training. The mere thought scared him. Finally, he decided to let her wake up on her own, no matter when that would happen. He was willing to take the blame if Blockhead got angry, so he might as well let her get the rest she needed.

Jenif! Jenif! Wake up, Jenif, or you will be late.

Her eyelashes fluttered until she managed to open her eyes. Without thinking, she asked what time it was, and Mark answered it was close to half past six already and that they should hurry. At first, she thought it was Blurreydal who answered, so when she looked around and saw the boy next to her, she let out a short scream of surprise just as he was looking at her in confusion.

'What are you doing here?' she suddenly asked, but before he could answer, she looked around the room and realised it wasn't hers. It took her a moment to remember how she ended up there, but when she did, she lowered her guard with a sigh of relief. 'Oh, I'm sorry.' The boy smiled in amusement as he was watching her.

'We should get ready for training, and we'd better hurry too!' he said and Jennifer nodded, but when she got up, she just stood there, not even blinking. 'What's wrong?'

'My training clothes are in my room...' The boy suddenly started laughing. When he calmed down, he answered her.

'Normally, you should go back to your room and get ready, but seeing that there's no time to waste, I'll let you wear my clothes today.' He couldn't stop smiling. 'I can't wait to see how funny you'll look in my clothes though!'

'Stop laughing, it's not funny. I bet I look stunning in your clothes,' she told him, smiling so much that her cheeks hurt. Meanwhile, Mark lent her some clothes that would probably fit her.

'These should work fine, they're the smallest I've got.'

As she thanked him, she made her way to the bathroom to get changed. In the mirror, she could only see a red-faced Jennifer with messed up hair. Once she splashed some water on her cried out face and got changed, she went out and asked Mark if he happened to have a comb she could use, but right then she caught him while he was putting on his shirt, and couldn't finish her sentence. On the other hand, Mark didn't seem at all bothered, unlike the girl, and actually started laughing at the sight of her in his clothes with that messy hair, making things a little bit more awkward for her.

The green t-shirt he gave her seemed huge on her, almost as long as a short dress, and the black trousers were far too long. She looked as if she was shrinking while the clothes were getting larger. The only thing that fit her, but now seemed out of place, was Blurreydal as a blue bracelet on her hand. The boy just couldn't stop laughing. Eventually, when he started to calm down, he said, 'you could probably use a comb, I might have one lying around,' and he made his way to the bathroom, passing a frozen Jennifer who was still shocked from her earlier sight and of a very awkward moment they somehow avoided.

Finally, she managed to turn around and thank him as he gave her a comb. While minding her hair in front of the mirror, she rhetorically asked, 'so, how do I look?'

'You look like you could use a tailor,' he said full of joy, which made the girl let out a laugh. 'Hm...I might have some scissors lying around too...'

The girl's eyes widened. 'My hair's fine, no need to cut it!' she said all of a sudden, which made Mark laugh more than ever.

'I wanted to shorten the trousers, but if you like them this long, I don't mind. At least I'll get the chance to pick you up when you fall!' His answer made her blush, and all she could say was 'oh'. Once he found those scissors, she let him cut the trousers so they'd be ankle-length.

Once he finished, she said, 'you just ruined some good trousers for me.'

'It was worth the sacrifice,' he said as the girl blushed once more. 'Back to reality now, let's hurry, we're late already. I hope you're ready,' and with those words he took her hand and sprinted to the cafeteria for some quick breakfast. Before she had time to complain, he told her that it was already seven, the time they were supposed to be in the training hall.

Eventually they reached the training hall, and they were only about a quarter of an hour late. However, when they got in, they stumbled upon a mad looking Blockhead.

16

Jealousy on the Go

To their surprise, their trainer started laughing instead of shouting.

Mark and Jennifer looked at each other in confusion, asking with their eyes what was wrong with Blockhead this time. He was *never* joyous, and rarely ever smiled at all, but laugh... that might as well have been a dream. A moment later, the two realised what could've passed through his mind to make him go from such an angry mood to one so happy, and their eyes turned wide.

'I see what happened here,' said Blockhead in amusement, to which the two automatically shouted in unison 'it's not what it seems!' However, they couldn't prove it, so they didn't even try to explain how the girl ended up in boy clothes. 'You never stop surprising me, kids. But who am I to interfere with your personal lives?' He quickly sighed, returning to reality, and continued: 'Just get to your training since you're finally here.' With those words he left.

As soon as Blockhead couldn't hear them anymore, the girl let out a very big sigh, asking herself 'how am I going to explain this to everyone?'

In return, the boy just put a hand on her shoulder and suggested something. 'Say all your clothes got dirty, and you needed to borrow some,' he said with a faint smile.

I bet he's enjoying the situation, the girl thought.

Jenif, don't say that! If anyone will get in trouble, that's him, not you, joined in Blurreydal.

Why is he so happy about it then?

Hm...I think he does it to cheer you up, not because he really is happy. But he did seem quite happy earlier, Blurreydal giggled.

Blur...Oh, you're right. Then, for Mark's sake, she smiled. 'Very well then, sounds like a good excuse to me, thanks Mark.'

He seemed to blush for a second. 'Anytime, Jen!'

From that point onward, they just had training as usual. Other than a few remarks on the girl's new outfit, nothing special happened. To her surprise, Mark's excuse really worked, and people stopped mocking her. However, she still got more attention than she would've liked, along with a couple of suspicious looks. Being in Blockhead's attention suddenly felt like a great thing, although it wasn't at all. Jennifer hated when the spotlight remained on her for too long.

One way or another, training ended, and the girl rushed to her room to get changed into *her* clothes; she couldn't wait. However, when she took Mark's clothes off, she suddenly felt a great warmth leave her, as if the clothes were some means for the boy to hug her continuously without even being there at all. 'I'll miss wearing these clothes,' she sighed.

Maybe Mark will let you keep them? suggested Blurreydal.

'Don't be silly Blur, I can't keep them.'

The little alien seemed confused. *Why not, Jenif?*

'Because...Because they're his, not mine!' she said, maybe a little too harsh. The blue alien, still a bracelet, wouldn't add anything anymore; the girl was too tense. 'Let's go over his room and return them,' she added in a low voice just as she was packing them nicely.

To her surprise, she stumbled upon Peter halfway. Apparently, he was going to her room to ask about the new clothes. Just as expected, she told him the same thing about not having any clothes left herself, so she borrowed some.

'Jenny, you're wearing your own clothes now in case you haven't realised. And anyway, I knew you were lying. Just tell me whose clothes those are and why did you need them,' the boy said. Peter looked at her expectantly but she didn't know what answer to give. Finally, she sighed and told him as briefly as possible.

'They're Mark's clothes,' she started, just as he let out a short 'humph' and frowned. 'It's a long story...'

'I have time.'

'Well, this morning I woke up very early, and thought of going over to apologise for some things. Apparently he was awake, so we stayed inside and talked. Soon I realised I was still sleepy and kind of fell asleep,' she said as she looked at the ground. The girl wouldn't mention the crying part. 'Nothing else happened, I promise!' she shouted, looking back at him.

'Go on,' he said when the girl stopped talking for a longer while. His voice was harsh and demanding; he wouldn't give up until he found out the whole story.

'When I woke up, it was already late,' she continued, and from that point, she told the story whilst looking at the floor. 'And since it was late, I didn't have time to go and get my own training clothes, so Mark suggested I borrow some of his.'

'So, he suggested it? And you accepted just like that?'

'Well, yes. I didn't have much of an option, so I accepted.'

'I see... So that's it?'

'That's it,' she repeated silently, still looking at the floor. 'And I don't see why I have to report to you anyway. Now if you'll excuse me, I have to give them back,' and without another word or response from Peter, she walked past him and reached Mark's room in a couple of minutes. On the way, she made sure Peter wasn't following her, and to her surprise, he wasn't.

Once she reached his door, she knocked and immediately got an answer from inside, saying 'it's open', so, naturally, she went in.

The girl felt very awkward for intruding his privacy and seeing his exposed chest. *Why does this keep happening?* However, Mark seemed quite amused, and said 'I just said it's open, not that you could enter.' To that, the girl grumbled a couple of words under her breath, 'You could've at least warned me,' but to which he gave no attention. To make matters worse, he forgot about putting on that shirt he was going to, and shifted all his attention to the girl. 'I see you already brought back my clothes. I thought you might want to keep them,' he said, but she shook her head.

'No, no, they're yours,' she managed to say, but was so shocked that she couldn't even blink. The boy took them from her hands since she was too frozen to hand them to him herself. To Jennifer's surprise, he unpacked them instead of putting them back in their places. Without any explanation, he held up the trousers and just looked at them and sighed.

'You might at least keep these ones, since I cut them short for you,' he said, still looking at the piece of clothing.

'I...I couldn't,' she managed to make out, and the boy raised an eyebrow. 'I mean...They're your clothes, I can't keep them. Even if you cut them to fit my length, they're still too large. Just...just keep them as a memory.' The boy couldn't help but smile at her words, so he finally gave in.

'Fine, just because you asked me so nicely.' In her mind, she was actually a little disappointed that she wouldn't get to feel the warmth of his clothes anymore, but she couldn't afford to let that show. She did the right thing.

After a few moments of silence, the girl returned to reality and thanked him before leaving. To her surprise, he took hold of her hand once she turned around, and pulled her closer into a tight embrace. She was so surprised that she couldn't even react. When she felt his warm skin wrapped around her, she couldn't help but put her head on his shoulder and let the hug surround her. After a minute, Mark slowly let go and whispered 'I'm sorry,' but to his surprise, the girl said 'it's okay,' so he tightly hugged her once more before letting go.

Smiling, she looked at him once more before leaving without another word. This time, the boy didn't even try to stop her.

When she got out, she met none other than Peter again, so she inquired, frustrated, 'what now?'

'What took you so long to give him back those clothes?'

'Go ahead and ask him. It's not like it's any secret now,' she said in as much a mean way as she could muster, and left him there without another word. As expected, Peter went in and asked Mark about everything. *I just hope he put on that shirt already,* she thought a little doubtful as she returned to her room.

Peter is jealous, said the little alien.

Whatever.

***

'Tell me what's happening?'

'What are you talking about?'

'You and Jenny, there's something happening and I don't like it.'

'You never like anything that's got to do with us two.'

'True that, but this time it's different, so tell me what's happening!'

Mark sighed. Peter wouldn't ever stop bugging him unless he found out what happened that day. To Peter's astonishment, the boy told him the exact same story about how the girl ended up with his clothes for the day, avoiding the crying part. Of course, Mark thought it while talking, but skipped it for Jennifer's sake.

'It's the same story Jenny told me...'

'So, you came here because you didn't believe her,' Mark added.

'It didn't seem believable. You can't blame me! But that wasn't the only reason I came here. I just wanted to see where she was going,'

'So, you followed her?' Peter nodded. 'Well, since that is dealt with, I think we can return to our lives.'

When he realised that he was being kicked out, he grumbled under his breath on his way to the door, and left without a word. Instead, he was constantly thinking *liar, liar, liar.*

From then on, every day at training they would do their best to avoid each other, to the point where they would act like strangers. This would continue for too long, and was already sickening. Once she realised this a few days later, Jennifer thought: *What have I done?*

17

Another Piece of the Puzzle

A week passed since Jennifer first encountered Blurreydal. She expected this day to be far different from the others, so she kept an eye open for anything out of the ordinary.

Today was the day when another alien companion ought to appear after someone was saved from death. That is, if the pattern remained the same. The tough part was finding that person.

What are the chances that it will be someone I already know? There are so many men here.

Low chances, answered Blurreydal.

Please don't let it be Zack, anyone but him! Well, maybe not Peter either, he's becoming...unpredictable. It could get dangerous...

Do not worry, Jenif. My kind knows how to pick, it will be a person who is reliable, you will see.

Hearing Blurreydal's words, Jennifer smiled, until she

remembered she was in the middle of a swordfight with Leonard. It turned out he was a much better swordsman than brawler, so he put up one good challenge for the girl.

Just as her mind shifted back to the present, her opponent managed to break through her guard and aimed for the feet. Before she could react, she ended up with a small, but deep cut on her left ankle. 'Ow, that hurt!' Her opponent just smiled back at her in sympathy. That would leave her limping for the rest of the day for sure. *Blur, help me end this quicker.* With a sudden burst of energy and power, the girl slashed once more at Leonard, and even though he managed to block, her blow was so powerful it overwhelmed him. With that, the girl won. *Thanks Blur.*

At the end, the two of them politely shook hands. 'You're a challenging swordsman, Leo. I'm looking forward to practicing with you again.'

'Could say the same about you, young lady. I don't know how you do it, but you always manage to take me by surprise. Makes me want to be a girl myself!' The two of them started laughing.

'Anyway, I have a favour to ask of you. Can you help me to that bench over there? You sort of gave me a good cut on my ankle, and I don't think I can jump my way there on my own.'

'Oh! Of course,' he said, and let her put one hand around his neck for support and jumped on her good leg the whole way. Carefully, the boy helped her sit down. 'There you go. Need some company until you feel better?' he politely asked. Just as politely, Jennifer refused, saying she was fine.

Once Leonard left, the girl was watching a brawl since

she was right next to a sparring circle. The ones fighting were Peter and another guy she didn't know personally, but only saw around every now and then. Just as the girl expected, Peter didn't give her any attention, and not because he was too busy or because he hadn't seen her there. Ever since the incident with Mark's clothes, he avoided her as much as he could. It was ridiculous. Either way, at the moment he was busy fighting, and apparently winning too.

While she was watching them, the girl heard footsteps nearing her, and a tall and broad person stopped right in front of her, watching the fight. 'Enjoying the show?' the person asked. The voice was low and serious, as ever. The person was obviously the one and only Blockhead.

'Um, I think so, sir.'

'I'm guessing this isn't your reason for staying here then?'

'Indeed, sir. I can't stand up because I've got a bad cut on my left ankle.'

'Theoretically speaking, this shouldn't stop your hands. You might as well do some weightlifting, Jennifer. You're a good enough swordsman for now anyway.'

'I appreciate the suggestion sir. I will find someone to help me to the weight corner as soon as I may.'

The trainer nodded. Jennifer was pleasantly surprised that he didn't get at all angry about her sitting down during training, and even complimented her swordsmanship! That rarely ever happened, so the thought made her happy.

A minute passed, and the two didn't say anything, but only watched how the fight went on in the sparring ring. It took a surprisingly long while. Peter had the upper hand because of his experience and strong build, but the other fighter didn't seem to give up, no matter what. It was certainly an interesting fight. At some point, Jennifer couldn't hold her curiosity anymore.

'Sir, if you don't mind me asking, who is that boy?'

'You're talking about the one Peter is fighting, the one with that strange red band around his head?' the girl nodded. That boy indeed did have a red band around his head, tied up to the side, which made him look funny, but definitely interesting. 'If I'm not mistaken, his name is Blake. Why do you need to know?'

'Mere curiosity,' she answered, watching that red band around his head. Where had he got it from, she wondered.

Before leaving her, Blockhead reminded her about the weightlifting. She didn't forget, but needed to see who won the fight first. Both fighters seemed exhausted, and she expected either of them to fall to their feet at any second. However, they managed to hold on somehow. To Jennifer, it seemed that Peter would win because he was much stronger than the other guy, Blake, who seemed so much thinner and a bit shorter in comparison. Blurreydal seemed to agree, and as the two of them mentally debated on how much longer they would last, Blake suddenly did something unexpected which caught her attention. He screamed and charged at Peter head first, just like a maddened goat, aiming for the stomach. The idea seemed crazy, because Peter was much stronger and heavier, and normally, that wouldn't even shake him. Now, however, whatever Blake's plan really was, it worked, because Peter fell on his back with a loud *thud*, remaining there, gasping for minutes. The few people watching, including Jennifer, clapped and cheered for the winner.

To her surprise, Blake passed right by her, but stopped when she called out 'wait a minute!'

'Yes?' she said as he turned around to face her, and then added, 'ohh, you're the famous Jennifer, aren't you? My excuses, mademoiselle.' She blushed for a second.

'And you must be Blake, am I wrong?' she added. He let out a tired smile.

'Indeed, that's my name. What can I do for you?'

'I just wanted to congratulate you on your victory. To be honest, I didn't expect you to win the fight, I know how tough Peter is during brawling... It was certainly an impressive fight. There must surely be more about you than you let show,' she said, trying to sound polite. When the boy didn't know what to say other than a short 'merci', the girl added, 'I like your head band by the way. It sure catches the eye.'

'It's wonderful, isn't it? It's my first day wearing it.'

'First day you say?' The girl raised an eyebrow. She had a feeling of déjà vu.

'Exactement, I found it in my room this morning. I'm guessing someone left me a present...'

'The same about my bracelet...' she said in a low voice, showing him the bracelet. It seemed to make him curious. After a short pause to think, he continued:

'I mean no disrespect, mademoiselle, but may I ask you to meet me at the cafeteria tomorrow morning?'

'Sounds great, see you there.'

Without another word, but with a short and polite bow,

the boy turned around to leave. That was when Jennifer remembered that she couldn't walk on her own, and was expected to do some weightlifting.

'Uh, Blake?' He stopped and looked behind his shoulder to see her. 'I could use a little help to get to the weight corner, I can't walk on my own right now. Mind lending me a hand?'

'Certainement, mademoiselle,' he said just as he was helping her get up. On the way, he asked how she got the cut on her ankle, so she told him all about it, and finished her story just as they reached their destination.

'Thanks, Blake, I owe you one.'

'Mon plaisir, mademoiselle.' He bowed again, and as he turned around to leave, he added 'à demain!'

Confused, Jennifer softly said 'um, same to you...' *What did he just say?* she asked Blurreydal as she was already starting some exercises.

I do not know. That was not alien, I understand naught of it. Maybe it's primitive humane speech.

Well, it sure sounded alien to me! exclaimed the girl, and they both started giggling.

***

Time passed and it was time she left the training hall for today. However, her left foot was numb, so she still couldn't use it to walk. At least the wound had clotted a while ago.

'How am I supposed to go talk with Caliban if I can barely walk?'

Suddenly, her saviour appeared at the worst time, as he

heard her talking to herself. Mark was obviously curious what it was all about, but didn't let it show.

'Hey, Jen. You look like you could use a lift.'

'I sure do, you came right in the nick of time. I thought I'd remain here on my own until morning.'

'Good to know I can be of help, where do you want to go?'

The girl took a moment to answer, because she first thought about what would happen if she asked him to take her to Caliban's, so she quickly said, 'to my room of course!' to which he nodded without complaint. He would find out what her affairs with Caliban were when the time came.

Without further ado, he raised her up from the ground, holding her as if she were just a small child.

'Woah!' she exclaimed, half laughing. 'I just needed some support. I can jump on my right leg just fine.'

'I just thought of making things more comfortable for you,' he said with a wink, and then added, 'and fun too.'

As soon as he finished his sentence, he started sprinting through the training hall, along the corridors and all the way to the girl's room. Without even thinking, she held her hands around his neck so she wouldn't fall, and cried out with joy the whole way, regardless of the puzzled looks of the rest of the people on the corridor.

Once they were in front of Jennifer's room, Mark put her down, helping her stay upright.

'Thanks for the ride, it sure was fun!' she laughed, and gave him a quick hug, trying her best not to lose her balance since she was standing on just one foot.

'I'm glad you think so,' he smiled proudly. 'Are you sure

you'll be alright though? If there's anything I can help you with, just let me know,' he assured her.

'I'll be fine, my room's not that big, so I don't think I need help walking around there too!' she giggled and thanked him one last time before entering her room.

Once she closed the door, she said out loud, 'Now wasn't that fun! Makes me hope I won't be able to walk more often from now on, ha ha ha!' she exclaimed.

This is both scary and cute, Jenif, kindly said Blurreydal.

18

Three is Better than Two

The following morning, Jennifer could walk on her own again. However, not without limping a little. As quickly as she could manage, she got dressed and left for the cafeteria.

I wish I could run. I'd save so much time! she thought.

Once she reached her destination, the girl saw Blake waving for her to join him. When she saw him, she noticed another person in front of him at the same table, but couldn't figure out who that person was because he was standing with his back to her. All she saw was black hair.

As quickly as she could, she got some food and went over to the two boys' table. As she neared the table, she noticed a tattoo on the black-haired boy's neck. *That's clearly Caliban,* she thought, astonished. This morning, the tattoo was in the shape of a piece of puzzle. Once she reached the boys, she sat down in between them, seen that the table was round.

'Good morning Blake, Caliban,' she said as she sat down.

'Hello Jennifer,' the two boys said in unison, after which Blake continued. 'Wait, you two know each other?'

'We do, just for a week though,' the girl answered.

'So, how's your ankle?' asked Blake, to which the girl answered that it was much better and that she could walk on her own.

Turning to Caliban, Jennifer asked, 'Did you tell him yet?' to which he nodded.

'So,' Blake joined in, 'what now?'

The three of them looked at each other without saying anything. Nobody knew what was supposed to happen next. Eventually, the girl spoke, 'First of all, I'd like to know your story,' she started, but when Blake looked at her in confusion, she continued, 'you know, how you got to meet your friend. In my case, I was close to death in a hospital ward. When I woke up, I was in my room with Blur. In Caliban's case, he was falling from a dangerous height which should've killed him, and then woke up with Smotch in his room. So, what's your story?'

For a moment, the boy looked down at his food, trying to remember what happened. After almost a full minute, he started talking:

'I think...I think that I was outside. Yes, that's it. I went outside after nightfall because I needed some fresh air.' Jennifer and Caliban gulped at hearing his words. Everybody knew that after nightfall, the security is activated, and that meant that if the sensors felt any movement, the security instantly killed it. 'The next thing I remember was that I was in my room, terrified by Sangier, who is now my red headband, and my new best friend,' he said smiling.

'Sangier, you say? That's an interesting name,' noticed the girl.

'Actually, I just call him Sange,' added Blake.

'Anyway, back to the point,' joined in Caliban. 'Our little friends were sent here with a reason. We have to find a way to work together to stop this war among our people and theirs. The problem is how do we do that?'

'Maybe,' started Blake, 'just maybe, if we could make our leaders see that *they* are not our enemies, they will make peace. But of course, they won't listen to our words, so we have to find a way to prove it.'

'In a way, *we* are the proof.' All eyes were on Jennifer. 'Just think of it. Who was it that saved our lives? *They* never meant to harm us, did they? In fact, *they* brought us back to life. Why would *they* do this if we were their enemies?'

'You have a point, Jennifer,' said Caliban. 'It's a good start, but we need more than this to make our leaders realise that *they* mean us no harm. Like Blake said, mere words won't make them believe us. And who knows what they'll do to us if we just go and tell them all we know? If they don't accept it, which I bet they won't, they will think of us as traitors and punish us; they could even kill us if they wanted to. We have one chance only, so we ought to choose our course of action wisely.'

The three of them looked down as if they could already feel the bitter taste of defeat. 'We're getting nowhere...' murmured Blake, until Jennifer cut him off.

'But what if we don't talk to them directly, but through a hologram? They wouldn't be able to punish us in that case, and we'd still get the message through.'

'The idea is not bad, but I see two problems here,' noted Caliban. 'First, how are you going to get a hologram which can also record speech? As far as I know, such a thing hasn't been created yet. And second, say you manage to get that hologram, they'll be able to see your face and track you down. The punishment will only be postponed, not avoided.'

'I've already thought of this. About the existence of such a hologram, it's no problem, because the scientists are already working on the H4K, meaning a message hologram. Right now, it's in Alpha stage, so we can't get on with our plan just yet. However, once it's ready and working, I'll be able to get my hands on it.' The boys looked at the girl puzzled, so she continued, answering the two boys' obvious question *how will you get it?* 'I know someone who can help me,' she said with a wink.

'What about the second problem?' asked Caliban.

'That's the easy part. One of us has to record the message, disguised. Of course, it can't be me because I'm the only girl around. It would be far too obvious who recorded it.' She took a break from talking to inspect their reactions. They both nodded, so she continued. 'I was thinking it should be you, Caliban. Half the guys here have black hair, like you, so it would be impossible to find the right one. You could wear some sunglasses so they don't see your eyes, and maybe wear something with a collar so it can partially cover your neck.'

The boys were very thoughtful, looking at each other. None

of them would dare talk yet, and didn't even know what to make of the girl's idea. Caliban thought of protesting about him being the one to record the message, but since he had no better idea, he wouldn't refuse to go for it. Eventually he murmured, 'I don't really like this idea, but I'll do it, since that was good reasoning.'

Soon, after thinking the plan through a couple of times, Blake joined in, excitedly: 'Quelle idée! This is bound to work.' His little comment made the girl let out a quick smile, who then stood up.

'Very well then, leave the first part of the plan to me, and I'll keep you updated with everything I find out. In the meantime, you think of other things we could do, and see if anything or anyone can help us.'

'Of course, mademoiselle,' said Blake waving goodbye at her as she turned around to leave for the training hall.

What the girl didn't know was that Mark had been watching her that morning, wondering what she had been discussing with Caliban and Blake for so long. Once he noticed she left the cafeteria, he went after her, trying to catch up, but only managed to do so after her reaching the destination. *Even when limping, she walks quickly!* he thought.

Once inside, he lost sight of her and sighed. He thought about where in the training hall Jennifer could have gone; she would be somewhere she doesn't have to put effort on her feet. Almost instantly he figured out her destination was the weight corner, where he had found her the previous day. Unfortunately, on his way there, he was stopped by his trainer.

'Get warmed up, Mark. I'll put you in a swordfight later.

I need you to teach one of the trainees a couple of moves by sparring him. Afterwards you're dismissed.' The boy sighed when he heard Blockhead's words, and murmured only for himself to hear, 'let's get this over with.'

Only two hours later he was done helping that person with the sword fighting and was free to do whatever he wanted, even leave the training hall early. Of course, his first destination was the weight corner. He was dead curious and eager to find out what Jennifer had been discussing with those two boys in the cafeteria that morning.

'Hey, Mark,' she quickly greeted him with a smile.

'Hi, Jen. How's your ankle?' *How am I supposed to bring up the subject?*

'It's much better now, I can walk again, although not as well as before.'

'I'm glad, but I guess this means you'll be getting no more lifts,' he said winking. *Just ask directly.*

'That's too bad, but walking on my own sure is great!'

'Indeed,' he answered, not knowing what more to say. When the girl saw he would say no more, she opened another subject.

'So, what are you doing here? Did you come to train with me?'

'Actually, I'm done for today.' *Coward, just ask her already!*

'Oh? How so? Did Blockhead say you can leave already?' she inquired, confused.

'Exactly. I only came here to see you before leaving. I wanted to ask you something...' A couple of moments passed and he still didn't ask his question, so the girl rhetorically asked 'yes?' watching him full of curiosity. Eventually, he said, 'I noticed you had some company this morning at the cafeteria... I was just wondering if I missed anything of importance.'

'Oh, that...' she whispered, a little surprised. 'It wasn't anything important, I just made some new friends and we were talking about how tough training can be sometimes. How this war is consuming all of us.' She was looking at the ground while talking, so the boy noticed there was something she didn't want to tell him. Fortunately for her, he wouldn't insist too much on the subject.

'Right...I guess I'll be going then, unless you change your mind and need another lift,' he winked, which made her smile. Without another word, he left, wondering on the way back to his room, *what is she hiding from me?* After posing many such questions, he thought again of her reaction. *I just hope I didn't upset her...* He sighed.

19

Getting on with the Plan

For a whole week, nothing of importance happened. Everyone was minding their own business, surviving Blockhead's training hours and enjoying the afternoon sun.

Caliban and Blake spent much time together, discussing, and complaining, about the war, and getting to know better their alien friends, Smolther and Sangier, and especially about a particular alien species; 'their kind'. Yet, they felt there was more crucial information they weren't told about. They simply couldn't find the right questions to ask. Therefore, as much as they tried to make up more plans for helping in the making of peace, they couldn't come up with anything. Regarding the current plan, they both agreed to it and could think of no way to make it more efficient than it already was. However, Caliban still didn't like the idea of him being the one to record the message. Until then though, he would enjoy his time; as much as one could enjoy his time in the Warband Academy.

On the other hand, Mark wouldn't give up trying to figure out what the girl's affairs were with those two boys, but seeing that for almost a whole week she didn't spend any time with them, he wouldn't insist too much and minded his own business. That didn't make him forget though; he would find out sooner or later. Other than pondering this matter, Mark tried practicing his brawling skills for once, and got much better, although his body wasn't made for such fights, unlike Peter's. In the same way, Peter practiced his sword fighting. However, these two boys still avoided each other, and to Jennifer's surprise, they didn't spend so much time with her either. The three of them had become more and more distant.

As for Nico, he barely ever saw his friends from training ever since he moved to the laboratory, working as a trainee scientist. He never concerned himself with their problems, even if they met on the corridors; he always said he was busy and left right away.

However, one day Jennifer went looking for him.

'Hello,' she shyly said as she entered the lab. 'I'm looking for Nico, is he here?'

One of the scientists answered her that he was busy in the far end of the lab, but that she would be allowed ten minutes to talk to him. The girl thanked the incognito man and went searching for Nico, heading in the direction that she was told.

On her way, she passed many gadgets she couldn't make any sense of, both small and big, some moving, others motionless, probably not working at all. At some point, she saw a tiny robot at her feet, and nearly stepped on it. She noticed it had a tiny broom, sprays and solutions, everything one would need for cleaning. It certainly did its job very well, because the floor and even the walls and ceiling were sparkling white, a colour she would now dislike, since she thought she was going blind in that room. The lab was certainly not to her liking; she preferred the darkened atmosphere of the training hall, even if it had a mad Blockhead in it.

Eventually, she reached the far end of the lab after walking for a couple of minutes; it certainly seemed like a huge place on her first visit! Working on a very small device was Nico, who was sitting down on a stool, frowning every time he forgot to do something which should have finally made that little device work. He didn't even notice Jennifer, and was startled when she greeted him. After he calmed down, she asked him what he was working on.

'It still needs a name, but it's meant for scanning the environment, and then sending all the data here so it can be inspected by the scientists. It's creating a virtual reality if I can say so,' he said, but stopped when he noticed the puzzled look on the girl's face. 'Anyway, what brings you here? I'm guessing it's something important?'

'I need to talk to you, I have a very big and important request,' she said, her face graver than ever, so Nico figured out it really was important.

'If it's concerning my brother, there's nothing I can do about it, sorry.'

'No! Forget him, he's got nothing to do with this.' Suddenly the boy's eyes were filled with curiosity and wonder. What could she need from him? 'I heard that a new version of the holograms is in development... It's the message ones, right?' He nodded. 'I'll be needing one as soon as they're up and working, it's important.' Her eyes were begging him, but he stood silent for a long while before answering.

'You have no idea what you're asking for, Jennifer. What could be so important that you need something from the lab? And for personal use too.'

'I...I can't tell you,' she looked down, avoiding his gaze. 'You wouldn't understand. You just have to trust me, please,' she whispered. The boy sighed.

'I'm sure you have your reasons, and I respect that. I know you're a trustworthy person. However, I would've liked to know what your intentions were on this occasion before just doing such a thing. It could get me into real trouble,' he whispered. The girl remained silent. She failed. What made her think it would be so easy to get something she wasn't even supposed to know about? 'But,' the boy continued.

'But?' She looked up, with a hopeful glance.

'But I know your intentions were never to harm anyone. I assume you are trying to do something important, probably help in a matter of life and death, who knows. I can't promise you anything, but I'll see what I can do in getting my hands on one of them once they're up and working without having anyone notice. It can't take more than a week, maybe two in the worst case. I hope your matter is not that urgent. I'll keep you updated.'

'I don't know how to thank you, Nico,' she said, feeling relieved. 'I'd better go now before your fellow scientists kick me out by who knows what robotic means I'd rather avoid,' the girl pointed out, which made the boy smile.

'Alright then, see you around.'

***

After her visit, Jennifer went outside for some fresh air. She needed to calm down. *It's going to work, the first part of the task is done, now it doesn't depend on me anymore,* she kept reminding herself.

As she found herself a place on a bench to enjoy the good weather, she saw Blake in the distance. She waved over at him so he would come and stay with her.

'Hello, mademoiselle, enjoying the garden?'

'As much as the good weather, indeed. What about you?'

'Same story, but Cal's going to join soon. He should arrive any minute now.'

'That's great, I really had to talk with you two. Until he comes, tell me, how are you getting along with Sangier?'

'Better and better of course! He's got some exotic personality if I can say so, and is always helping me see the bright side of things. Plus, he looks amazing on my head,' he said, and the two started laughing. 'I wish everyone knew what amazing friends the aliens can be,' he sighed. Jennifer agreed.

The two continued talking until Caliban finally showed up from behind them, startling the girl with a sudden 'Boo!'

'Don't you ever do that again!' she threatened him as he lay down on the grass, laughing at her reaction. Smolther was showing a smiling face. After a couple of moments of being angry, the girl started laughing too, Blake along with them.

Eventually, Caliban stopped laughing since he was out of breath, stood up and sat himself on the bench next to Jennifer and Blake.

'So, what did I miss, guys?' he asked as he joined his hands behind his head, watching the clear sky.

'Jennifer and I were just talking about Sange and Blur while we were waiting for you to come.'

'That's right,' added the girl. 'I have something to tell you two, good news.' The boys seemed delighted, and were especially glad to know that the first step in their mission was completed, and successful.

'So, I guess all we can do now is wait,' concluded Caliban who was still watching the sky, not moving from that position. 'How long? Up to two weeks? Awesome, I have time to prepare my speech. Blake, you find me some awesome glasses! Make sure they're big and black like my hair,' he said, and then they started laughing, not just because it was funny, but also for the sake of being joyful.

The three of them continued talking about happy random things for another ten minutes or so. Suddenly, Mark appeared next to them, eager to know what was so funny.

'Hi, Jen. Hello, Cal, Blake. What are you guys doing? You all seem so happy,' he said, sketching a smile.

'We were just making fun of Caliban's overgrown hair. I was thinking of tying up his hair with some of my hairbands, what do you think?'

Before Mark could answer, Caliban quickly protested, 'but that's going to make my head look like a palm tree orchard!'

'I'd like to see that,' laughed Mark.

'Me too,' joined in Blake. 'But I was thinking it would look more like a field of crazy geysers.'

'Stop making fun of my hair, guys!' he managed to say in between breaths. He was laughing so hard you could see tears rolling down his cheeks. 'Why don't we try tying up your hair, Jennifer?'

'Go ahead and try,' she answered. 'But it's going to look great however you do it!' To Caliban's disappointment, they all agreed on that.

For more than an hour, the four of them continued talking, never mentioning the alien friends in front of Mark. To make things even better, the boy stopped thinking that Jennifer was spending too much mysterious time with those two without wanting to tell him why. It all seemed so unimportant now.

Sooner than they thought, dusk was upon them, which instantly made Blake gulp.

'Guys,' he started. 'I think we'd better get inside quick, before the security is turned on!' The other three agreed, and rushed inside, racing. Of course, the girl was first since she was the fastest, second was Blake, because he was the most scared, third was Mark, who did his best to catch up with the girl, and last came Caliban, who never bothered on sprints.

Once inside, Jennifer said she was exhausted and that she was going to sleep. The boys agreed it was high time for some rest, and they all parted ways, eager to get a good night's sleep after a long day.

20
Reunion

The next day passed quickly, and so did the next and the one after. For almost a week, nothing special happened, until one day, Peter took Jennifer by surprise during training.

'Jenny, I've been looking all over for you!' he shouted from a distance, running up at her.

'Oh? What for? Did something happen?'

'I know It's not important, but I just wanted to show you my new sword fighting skills,' he said excitedly.

Jenif, he wants a Paiyle Grumm!

Then he shall have a good one. Blur, I'll go on my own on this one, I want to see exactly how good he is now.

As you wish, Jenif.

'A duel it is then,' the girl said with a cunning smile. She wouldn't lose so easily. *I hope he doesn't surrender after two cuts, that's going to be no fun.* 'Grab a sword!'

'May the duel start,' added Peter once he got himself his weapon.

Their duel didn't last for too long, but it was just enough for them both to become exhausted. Unfortunately, Jennifer never managed to get the upper hand and go on the offensive. She barely got one cut on Peter's thigh, and to her disappointment, it didn't even bleed much. On the other hand, she had gotten herself two small cuts on her feet, and a longer one around her right shoulder; at least none of them were deep, so they almost didn't bleed at all. However, she could barely stand up.

Cursed be his strength, I'm stuck defending and he's breaking all my defence with that brute force of his!

You are right, but he also learned how to move the weapon.

Very soon, the girl dropped her sword. All force left her arm from that long cut. She looked at Peter for a second before she fell down on her knees in surrender only to see his emotionless face. What was on his mind? His eyes showed neither pity, nor anger, nor friendship, nor anything else.

'Well done, you're the winner. You bested my skills, congratulations,' the girl whispered while catching her breath. She waited for Peter to say something, anything. In the meantime, she would stay down on her knees, breathing heavily.

Before daring to say a word, the boy looked behind his shoulder as if to check something. Only then he opened his mouth to talk: 'Zack, come out!' The girl's eyes went wide in a flash.

Blur, tell me what's happening!

Zack boy is coming behind you. Peter is just watching.

The girl's heart suddenly started beating quicker and quicker. Whatever Zack was doing there, it was not good, she was certain! She would've run away, but she was weakened; too weak to even stand up. She tried, however, but had a feeling there was some sort of poison on Peter's blade that made her so weak. Not even Blurreydal could help. All she could do was look up at the duel winner and pray with her eyes that nothing serious would happen.

As she looked in Peter's direction, she carefully watched what was behind him. *Where's Blockhead when you need him?* Of course, he was busy far away. So was everyone else she knew, and whoever was closer paid absolutely no attention. *Of course, that's why he looked back!* Now she was scared.

He is coming close! said Blurreydal.

Indeed, Zack was already next to her. He lowered himself down on one knee to whisper in her ear as he got hold of her hair so she wouldn't run away, even though she was paralysed:

'Don't worry, we're not going to hurt you,' he started, the girl let out a soft sigh of relief. 'Not yet.' Jennifer bit her lip so hard it was close to bleeding. Her throat seemed to burn, so she couldn't make out a sound.

What are they up to?

Without another word, they carried her out of the training hall as if she were no more than a human sized puppet. Everyone around probably thought that they were just helping her to the hospital. Of course, that everyone meant nobody she knew. She was on her own, defenceless and powerless.

Jennifer would've struggled, but that duel left her unable to defend herself. Peter was cunning; he had a plan from the beginning, and she just played the part he wanted her to. There was no point in even trying to shout for help either, since her throat was so tight it burned. Tears were silently rolling down her cheeks, things which the boys wouldn't take notice of.

Before she knew it, she closed her eyes and didn't open them until it was too late.

***

'Mark, have you seen Jennifer?'

'Not since breakfast, sir. Has anything happened?'

'I was keeping track of how many trainees are still here and how many should be. Three seem to be missing, and one is definitely her.' Mark gulped.

'But she must be here! She never leaves without approval, and I know she came today because I was with her,' he said thoughtfully.

'You seem content that she was here, and I am content that she's not anymore.' The young boy looked at the floor trying to think of a logical explanation, but in vain. For a minute, Blockhead was watching him in silence until he finally spoke again. 'Mark, I grant you permission to leave training early today if you want to go look for her.'

'Thank you, sir,' he whispered and left. He was slowly walking towards the exit, thinking of a destination.

She could be in her room, or maybe enjoying the good weather outside. Or maybe she just felt hungry and went back to the cafeteria. Where should I go first? Still, if she went to any of these places, it wouldn't explain her early departure; she never disobeys orders! I'm missing something...

As he was thinking of whatever could help him figure out where the girl had gone to, he stumbled upon two familiar, but worried faces. It was unmistakably Caliban and Blake.

'Mark, Mark,' Blake started shouting in desperation. 'Have you seen Zack? Blockhead put me to duel him, but he's nowhere to be found! If I don't find that guy quick, he'll think I ignored his orders!'

'Peter seems to have disappeared too. Leo was worried that he couldn't find him anywhere in the training hall, and when I helped him look for Peter, I realised he really was gone!'

Mark was digesting all the information. Blockhead mentioned three trainees being gone, out of which Jennifer. Now Caliban and Blake said that Peter and Zack are gone too, so that made three. *Coincidence? I think not.* Finally, he whispered so that just the boys could hear him, 'Jen's gone too. Blockhead said there are three missing...' Immediately the other two boys' eyes were wide open as they put the pieces of the puzzle together.

'We have to go look for her!' exclaimed Caliban. Everyone agreed.

'This could just be a coincidence though,' whispered Blake and then added, 'but we all know it's probably not, so let's go!'

'Where to exactly?' asked Mark, the most worried of all three.

'If those two freaks are involved, they must be in one of their rooms. Anywhere but in public,' suggested Caliban. The other two only nodded.

'That's where I'm going then!' quickly said Mark, already

ready to run as if his life depended on it, until the two boys caught him by the arm. 'What are you doing? Let go!' he furiously said.

'We're coming too!' they both protested.

'You're going to get in trouble if you leave training,' he quickly answered.

'We can explain tomorrow, forget about training for now,' said Blake. Mark only nodded and they all started running as fast as they possibly could.

***

'Peter's room is really close, we're going there first,' said Mark as he was running with Caliban and Blake following him closely. None protested.

When they finally reached Peter's room, they sneaked close and eavesdropped at the door before trying to enter; the door was bound to be locked anyway. Everything felt silent. If there was anyone inside, they didn't make a single sound. The room was most probably empty though, so they just checked to see if the door was by any chance unlocked before moving on. Of course, it wasn't open. There was always that small possibility that they were in there. However, they couldn't afford to linger any longer; they moved on.

'Next up, Zack's room.'

'I'll take the lead now,' joined in Caliban. 'I don't think you know where his room is.' Mark didn't protest.

They reached his room after five minutes of running at full speed. To Mark's astonishment, Zack's room was the last one on the northern Academy wing, so it took longer than expected to get there.

Once they reached the door, they sneaked close and eavesdropped before trying to get in. No clear sounds could be made out, but there were certainly *sounds*.

'Seems like there's at least two people inside. One voice is softer, must be Jennifer,' whispered Caliban.

As soon as he heard those words, Mark didn't wait and tried to force the door open, shouting 'open up, open up!' Before they realised it, the other two boys were helping him break down the door so they could get inside. From inside, no more voices could be heard; they were obviously shocked, maybe even scared.

It only took the three boys a couple of seconds to break down the door. Inside, they found none other than Zack, Peter and Jennifer, all of them looking at the intruders. The boys showed anger, the girl showed fear and hope. She was in a corner, both hands and feet tied up with rope, so she couldn't move. Also, her shirt was cut short to just above her belly button. Thin traces of blood covered her belly.

'Well if it's not prince charming trying to save his little princess,' mocked Peter, to which Mark just growled in frustration.

After a couple of moments of watching each other, Caliban whispered, 'Mark, you take care of Zack. We'll take care of Peter.' And so they did, having each other's backs. Whatever reason the kidnappers had to take Jennifer; it didn't matter; now they had to save her.

The boys carried on fighting, mostly harming the enemy

with their fists since they had no weapons. Caliban and Blake together managed to get the upper hand against Peter, but they couldn't get rid of him. In Mark's case however, none of them ever managed to have the upper hand; their brawling skills were equal. The girl could only watch in terror. At some point she screamed:

'Mark! Watch out, he's got a knife!' The boy's eyes went wide in shock. He had to be extra careful now; Zack was aiming to kill.

Before he realised it, his enemy got a knife from somewhere, and was desperately trying to hit Mark as he dodged his every attempt. However, he couldn't dodge a knife for too long. He needed to find a plan, and quick! On the other hand, his two allies quickly looked at each other and nodded. Without wasting another second, Blake threw himself on Zack while Caliban was holding his own with Peter wrath. At the impact, Zack fell down, very surprised. Luckily, he dropped the knife from his hand, so Mark quickly grabbed it.

Once down, Zack couldn't get up any longer because Blake was keeping his foot on his back. Zack was now KO. As quickly as he could, Mark rushed over to Jennifer and cut the ropes binding her feet and hands. As soon as her hands were free, she wrapped herself around his neck and let go of all the tears she had been holding in for so long. 'Thank you,' was all she managed to say.

'Let's get you out of here,' he said in return, but she didn't nod as expected.

'They took my bracelet. I have to find it first!' The boy didn't answer. He didn't understand why that bracelet was so important that she couldn't leave without it. From behind, Caliban shouted, asking what was taking them so long. 'They took Blur while I was unconscious!' she shouted in response, to which he gulped.

'Find it quick then. I don't think I can hold Peter much longer.'

'I can't hold Zack down either. He keeps struggling,' added Blake.

'Mark, help me find my bracelet!' the girl said in a hurry as she was already searching the room. The boy nodded.

'After this, you owe me some explanations.'

For a whole minute, the two of them looked everywhere for Blurreydal as Caliban and Blake kept shouting 'hurry!' over and over again. When she eventually looked in the bathroom, she found her little alien friend, still in the form of a bracelet. However, she found it curious that she couldn't reach for Blurreydal with her mind; not until she found him.

'Let's get out of here,' she finally said, so the four of them rushed out of the room before either Zack or Peter could stop them.

Before they allowed themselves to take a break to talk, they ran for minutes until they were certain that the two kidnappers and would-be murderers weren't following them. Eventually they got outside. Even if the two had been following them, they couldn't afford to try anything in public. Especially not against four at once. Jennifer finally felt safe. However, she was still crying.

As soon as they got outside, they all stood on the soft grass. The three boys tightly hugged her, telling her that it was alright now, that she was safe and that those two were dealt with. Still, they would let her cry in peace as much as she wanted and only wiped the tears off her face every now and again. When she stopped crying so hard, she managed to talk a little, although her throat felt so tight it hurt even to breathe.

'Zack meant to kill me...' The boys didn't know what to say. Eventually she continued. 'But before he would do it, he enjoyed torturing me. It was horrible! As he pulled back my hair, he kept that knife at my exposed neck. Every time I would be 'displeased' with him cutting my shirt shorter, he would push the blade harder against my neck. I had to let him have his way; there was nothing I could do with my hands and feet tied like that. They also poisoned me, to make me weak. And every time he cut my shirt shorter, he made sure he left a little mark on my abdomen too. This must have gone on for at least an hour. I thought I was done for!' She took a little break from talking, finding it hard to catch her breath. Meanwhile the boys looked for those cuts she was talking about. Indeed, her body was full of them, one next to the other. At least they weren't deep so they didn't bleed her out, but they were obvious and hurt the girl very much. It would take her a long while until she fully healed from that day. 'Peter never said anything,' she managed to make out a little later. 'He always watched as if his eyes were drugged with hatred, I think. I don't know what went through his mind, but whatever he felt, it wasn't shown on his face.'

That was all the girl managed to say. The boys were speechless still. All they managed to do was hug her to show that she was now safe. Through their minds, several common feelings passed by: shock, disgust, hatred and anger, all towards Zack and Peter. Eventually, Mark remembered something.

'As soon as you feel better, you'll have to explain why you went back for that bracelet,' he said, still wondering what made it so important.

'I'll handle the storytelling from here,' joined in Caliban, to which the girl nodded. 'We owe you an explanation, and you of all people have a right to know.'

Starting the story from the beginning, Caliban told Mark what happened ever since he 'died' and was brought back to life by the aliens. Although he didn't understand what this had to do with the bracelet, Mark didn't comment at all. Caliban mentioned everything that happened, in chronological order, until the present. He also included their plan to stop the war.

As soon as the story was told, Blake joined in saying, 'Welcome to the party!' to which they all smiled, even Jennifer. After a minute of silence, the girl managed to word out what each of them was thinking: 'So what now?' she asked.

'I guess,' answered Blake, 'that our priority is to let Blockhead know what happened to you because of those two. Then we should try to get on with our plan. You'll have to focus on healing, of course.' They all agreed. 'We can talk to Blockhead tomorrow morning at training.'

'Good idea,' enforced Mark, after which he added: 'Right now we should worry about Jen. I'm not going to leave her on her own anymore after what happened!'

'We'll help,' said Blake.

'That's right,' joined in Caliban. 'At night we can take turns watching over her room so that none enter, and during the day, at least one of us has to be with her.' None complained. It was a good idea, and they decided to stick to it.

'I'll take the first watch tonight,' offered Mark. 'One of you guys should come take my place a few hours later and so on until morning.'

Without complaint, they all left the outdoors since it was already getting late.

You will be alright, Jenif. The boys will take good care of you, said Blurreydal as they were walking back inside.

21

Action and Reaction

Mark was walking alongside the girl, going towards her room. She was still thinking of what had happened that day, and shivered every now and then. Other than that, she wouldn't even talk, and often watched the floor instead of looking forward. The boy stood silent himself.

Only when they reached her room they stopped in front of her door and looked at each other for a minute. Finally, Mark spoke.

'You go get some rest; I'll keep watch here.' She simply nodded and opened the door, ready to go inside. 'Um, Jen?' he suddenly added, so the girl turned back waiting for him to continue. 'Sorry for not getting there earlier.' He watched the floor to avoid her gaze. After a few moments, Jennifer spoke herself:

'It's ok. I couldn't even have hoped for anyone to find

me, much less rescue me. Thanks,' she said in no more than a whisper, adding a weak smile.

The boy only nodded and wished her a good night. Without another word, she went inside, and the boy let out an audible sigh, probably of relief. At the same time, the girl threw herself on the bed, crying herself to sleep.

For at least three hours, Mark stood in front of her door, keeping guard. Luckily, nobody passed, so nothing happened. At some point, when he started feeling tired, Caliban showed up and took his place. Several hours later, Blake came, taking Caliban's place. When Jennifer woke up and went out of her room, she stumbled over a yawning Blake. Without much talk, they went to the cafeteria and met with the rest of the group.

The boys did their best to cheer her up, talking about random things which didn't imply kidnapping or death, asking for the girl's opinion on something, or just trying to get her to talk and forget about what happened. Unfortunately, when Jennifer opened her mouth to talk, it was no more than a short sentence which often ended the discussion. Most of the time, silence ruled over their table.

Eventually, they finished breakfast and went to the training hall. Jennifer seemed the least excited of all, not that the others were eager to train either. In her case though, she was full of scars, bruises and other cuts all over her body, and every movement was painful. However, she tried not to let it show, and never mentioned it, although the boys knew she found it hard to even move.

A very unexpected thing happened then. Just as they entered the training hall, the girl was being squashed in a very tight hug. All she managed to make out was a very weak 'ow' while trying to figure out who was holding her, since her head only reached the person's chest. At some point, she managed to hear a faint whisper, barely audible at all, saying 'my girl,' but gave it no attention. She almost felt as if she were being swallowed as a whole while her skin was on fire. It wasn't a very pleasant feeling, but she figured out that whoever was holding her, did it out of compassion, not meaning to hurt her, so she didn't try to loosen the grasp. Finally, after what felt like an hour, whoever was holding her let go, and she had a look around.

First, she saw the boys' shocked faces, not daring to say a word or move a muscle, and then as she was searching for that person, the only one she found was none other than Blockhead. Even if she wanted or could say a word, she wouldn't. She was far too surprised and didn't even know what she could say anyway, so she just stood there dumbfounded, waiting for an explanation. In only a matter of seconds, that explanation came.

'It's great to see you're alright, Jennifer! I was worried sick when I noticed you were missing. I soon found out who else was missing, and I must say my heart skipped a beat. Also, when I saw Blake and Caliban leaving in a hurry alongside Mark, I figured something really did happen. You'll all have to explain to me in detail everything that happened yesterday, but for now I'm just glad you're fine.' He finally stopped talking, but the four of them were still watching him as if he was, for the first time ever, a human being with feelings. What they saw was a completely different side of Blockhead, one that nobody expected to even exist.

None of them planned on saying anything, but since an awkward silence filled the air, Caliban decided to handle the storytelling, mentioning every detail he could remember. As he was talking, their trainer's face was grave and full of surprise and confusion. On the other hand, the girl looked the other way, not daring to add a single word to the story; the memories were far too painful. Just for standing there, avoiding crying, she was very strong, although she always denied it. *I'm such a girl. I'm so weak.* Unfortunately, Blurreydal's words never seemed to comfort her.

Finally, the storytelling was over. Blockhead had a long look at the four kids before saying anything. He was now watching the girl with other eyes; eyes of pity and praise. Still, she looked anywhere else. Either way, the trainer started talking.

'Caliban, you mentioned that Zack had a knife, right?' The boy nodded. 'I wonder when he stole it from the dagger throwing corner. I should've noticed, I check them every day! No matter, he is a thief too, and for this his punishment shall be worse than Peter's,' he said.

'So, they're both being punished? What's going to happen to them?' inquired Mark.

'Indeed. I'm sending them to Correction School.' To those words, the boys eyed him curiously. They were all wondering where that was and why they never heard of it before. Blockhead figured this out, so he immediately answered their unspoken questions. 'I'm sending them away from the Warband Academy, past the gates,' he said as the boys' eyes turned wide. The girl was listening too, but didn't care what happened to those two monsters. 'Yes, there are things past the border, there is life and plenty of settlements. There are great hospitals, there's Correction School, the Spy Headquarters, and plenty of farms and factories where men unable or refusing to fight in the war are working, and helping in anyway they can. Where do you think all our food comes from? Anyway, this is not the time to talk about this matter. We'll leave it for another time.' The boys sighed in disappointment, but didn't complain. Jennifer still didn't look interested, but this time she really would've liked to know more, especially about the Spy Headquarters.

'So, the conclusion is that we won't be seeing them anytime soon,' pointed out Blake who restrained himself from yawning as much as possible. He was most tired of all, and everyone noticed.

'You got that right. As for you, kids, I have separate assignments for each of you. Jennifer, you are going to rest for a week. I don't want to see you in the training hall at all until the week is over. You must recover first... from all points of view.' Without waiting, she nodded and left. Mark offered to escort her to her room, but Blockhead quickly stopped him, so the girl went alone. 'I have something to discuss with only you three,' he said as soon as Jennifer was out of earshot. 'I see you're all tired... more tired than usual I mean. I'm guessing you're keeping guard at night instead of sleeping?' The boys nodded, surprised. *How did he guess?* they all wondered, although it wasn't so important. He probably figured it out from Blake's constant yawning. 'It is a noble thing to do.

Maybe she doesn't realise it, but that girl is very lucky to have true friends like you. For this and for your service yesterday, I'll allow you all to leave for today. Also, just so you don't end up falling asleep around here, you're free to come and leave the training hall at any hour, with the condition that you spend at least an hour doing intense training every day. Of course, until Jennifer heals. Afterwards, everything is returning to normal.' The boys nodded and thanked their trainer. It was definitely a very good deal, there was no refusing it. 'That is all, you're dismissed.'

'Goodbye, sir,' they said in unison as they turned around to leave.

As they were walking away, Mark suddenly asked the other two, 'Should we catch up with Jen and stay with her?'

'I think she needs a bit of time on her own,' answered Caliban. 'And anyway, those two are gone now, I don't think we have anything to fear. Also, she must be heading for her room, no danger there, and if she's heading for some other place, we'll see her around.' Caliban was right, so Mark agreed. Soon afterwards Blake suggested going outside to enjoy the good weather. Then he added, 'I heard that tomorrow it's going to rain heavily.'

Mark seemed to have other plans since he had remembered something. 'You guys feel free to go outside. I'll join you soon. I just remembered that plan you told me about. I'll go to the lab to check with my bro to see if there's been any progress on the H4Ks.' Caliban and Blake agreed, so they parted ways.

***

A couple of hours later, Mark finished talking with Nico and went outside to meet with the other boys. They were waiting eagerly for his arrival.

'So how did it go?' inquired Blake as soon as he saw Mark approaching them.

'Blake, you're too hasty,' joined in Caliban. 'But seriously now,' he added turning to Mark. 'How did it go?'

Seeing how anxious the two boys were, Mark couldn't resist but take a very long time before answering just for the sake of keeping them in suspense. Eventually, soon after Mark reached them, he answered.

'I got it,' and he showed a mischievous smile. Caliban and Blake were so excited that they started jumping around, asking how it worked, when they could see it and use it and so on.

'Just wait till Jennifer sees this! It will definitely cheer her up, I'm sure!' said Caliban.

'Let's go over and find out,' suggested Blake, to which they all agreed, and left for her room full of excitement.

Soon they were knocking on her door, waiting for her to open it. However, she still seemed to be in a bad mood, so all the boys managed to get out of her was 'I'm busy, leave me alone!'

'Jen, please come out, just for a second,' begged Mark. *Silence.* 'Please?' he tried again. *Silence.*

'We have a surprise for you,' added Caliban. 'You'll love it, I'm sure.'

'I don't want to see it,' she finally said.

'Why not? It will cheer you up!' tried Blake, but to no avail.

'I don't want to be cheered up,' she answered, so the boys sighed.

'Fine, we'll show you tomorrow at breakfast if you don't want to see it now,' said Mark, trying to stay positive. 'Sweet dreams,' he added, and the three boys left.

What they didn't know was the reason for why Jennifer refused to come out; she was a mess. Her face was all red and wet because of the crying, and her eyes were forming eye pouches from exhaustion. Her hair was all tangled and dirty, and her clothes were worn out. In spite of Blurreydal's constant tries of convincing her to get over the incident, she couldn't.

Also, other than crying, the girl had been thinking of two things, both regarding the scene from the training hall that morning.

The first thing was related to the other settlements they never knew about, like hospitals, the Correction School, farms, but especially the Spy Headquarters. She was determined to find out more about that as soon as she recovered, and if possible, visit the place herself. *Working as a spy would definitely be better, and safer, than fighting in the front lines. They hardly let me do anything at all anyway,* she thought. Blurreydal made no comments, and let the girl think whatever she wanted, whether it was right or wrong. It was only fair that she would find out herself.

The second thing was about two specific words someone said, although she was pretty sure that she had imagined it. When she suddenly found herself hugged by Blockhead that morning, she heard two words which she couldn't get out of her mind, and was certain that if anyone did say them, it was him. The words were 'my girl'. The problem was that she didn't know what to make of them, but was sure they weren't said randomly.

She had to think it over and over again before realising it; Blockhead saw her as a daughter.

22

Surprise Parting

Early the next morning, the boys were waiting eagerly for the girl to come out of her room and join them for breakfast. They were tired after having kept watch overnight.

'What if she's still sleeping? We shouldn't wake her up in that case, non!' whispered Blake, concerned like the other boys.

'I don't think she's sleeping though.' murmured Mark. 'She's better than that, I know her!'

'Then this can only mean she doesn't want to come out. I don't know what you think guys, but I don't want to make her more upset by forcing her to do anything,' added Caliban.

'You have a point.'

Slowly retreating from her door, they finally went to have breakfast...late breakfast anyway. Their plans for the day were to get some morning training before leaving and trying, hopelessly or not, to get Jennifer to face them and, if possible, talk. It sounded like a good enough plan.

The morning went quicker than the boys had first expected, so they left training with more energy than they had when they started. They were fortunate to not spend enough time there to get any bruises or scratches.

As quickly as they could manage, they went back to Jennifer's room, knocking and waiting for a response, but in vain. She wasn't even there.

'I wonder where she has gone off to...' murmured Caliban as he was scratching his chin in wonder. As the boys took a minute to think, Mark had an idea and burst out:

'I was thinking...' he started. 'Your alien friends communicate telepathically, right?' The two boys nodded. 'Maybe Smotch and Sange can ask Blur where they are?'

'This should work out well... what do you say, Smotch? Can you do this for us?' asked Caliban. As an answer, the little black tattoo on his neck changed to illustrate confirmation. Minutes later, he repeated what Smolther was telling him. 'He says it's hard to reach for Blur. They must be far away, but still he managed to get a few words...something like *must be alone...far off...going soon.*'

'What is that supposed to mean, 'going soon'? She's not leaving, is she?' said Blake, worriedly. The three boys looked at each other in astonishment.

'She can't leave the Academy without Blockhead's approval, can she? And he can't approve of this! Why would she leave anyway, and where would she go? And without telling us?' kept questioning Mark as he was walking in circles. Of course, all of them were shocked by this sudden change of tides, but he seemed the most affected of all. 'It's got to be a misunderstanding!' he snapped as if arguing with himself and started doubting whether those alien 'friends' were any good after all.

'Calm down, Mark!' shouted Caliban in order to get his attention. 'We will go see Blockhead and sort things out.'

'But...but what if she does leave? I...*we* will lose her forever, and what about our plan with the hologram? How are we going to restore peace if she's leaving?'

Blake put his hand on Mark's shoulder trying to calm him down and stop moving in circles. However, his fingers never stopped fiddling. 'Keep calm, man! Supposedly she did leave, which I'm sure she won't, she wouldn't want us to fail our mission, with or without her. Either way, it's going to be alright.'

'Thanks for the speech, Blake,' joined in Caliban, 'but can we go and see Blockhead already?'

'You're right, let's go.' He sighed.

Soon they were back to the training grounds and found their trainer there, keeping watch of every single detail. The only thing that slipped his vision was their arrival, so he was surprised to see them back.

'Well hello young gentlemen. I don't suppose you came back for training?' inquired Blockhead, quite pleased, so Caliban took a step forward and started speaking.

'Actually, no, sir. We only just heard rumours that Jennifer is planning to leave, where we don't know. We wanted to know if that is true.'

'Indeed, she did come earlier today to ask me about it. She

wants to move to the Spy Headquarters, but don't ask me why.'

'You aren't granting her permission for such a thing, are you, sir?' he asked with begging eyes.

'I must admit I would feel very sorry for not having her under my watchful gaze any longer, but alas! She has her liberty to try out whatever she pleases and learn from her mistakes. Therefore, I did grant her permission to go, but I doubt she'll stay there for too long a time; I'm sure she'll come back realising she's not meant for this sort of change.'

The three boys were shocked, almost breathless, watching Blockhead as if he were a ghost talking to them. Their expressions were so obvious that their trainer noticed quickly and continued talking.

'I suppose this is hard for you to swallow up. Didn't she tell you anything?'

'She won't even see us, ever since…the incident,' added Blake before Mark cut in with a very low voice, watching the ground:

'When is she leaving?'

'This I cannot tell exactly. I told her she can start packing only after she's fully healed, which is going to take a while as you very well know.'

'I just hope she doesn't plan on leaving earlier…'

'Oh, no, this is not possible. She cannot get out of the Academy grounds without my assistance. Jennifer will be needing an escort coming from the Spy Headquarters to fetch her. There's no way she's leaving before I clear all that up.'

The three boys sighed in relief.

'So, we still have time to talk her out of it, that's great!' said

Mark, getting excited. 'Thank you very much, sir.'

'One more thing before you leave, boys!' The three of them turned back in wonder. 'You do realise that either of you, even all if so you wish, can go as well. She is not the only one with the right for a change,' he winked.

'We will have to think about it,' said Mark a little in doubt. 'Have a nice day, sir.'

'See you tomorrow, boys.'

***

An hour later, the three boys were resting on a bench outside the Academy, enjoying the fresh air. Although the sky wasn't sunny today because of the clouds, the cool air refreshed them and helped them think clearly.

'I can't believe she isn't here either,' said Mark all of a sudden, breaking the silence that had been ruling for a while. 'Where could she be?'

'I was wondering something else,' joined in Caliban in somewhat of a reverie. Blake and Mark were already looking at him curiously. 'Right before we left, Blockhead said we could go to the Spy Headquarters ourselves. I don't know about you, but I'm really thinking of this as an opportunity. And then we'd shoot two birds with one stone...or me anyway. Trying something new and keeping an eye on Jennifer at the same time.'

'Caliban, I'm not saying you're wrong. On the contrary, you're very right, but not in my case. Even if I did go, they would kick me out at the very sight of me. Do you see me as a spy?'

Thinking this was a tricky question, so he only managed to answer with 'Why not?' to which he got a long set of 'because' arguments.

'I'm the least sneaky person you'll ever meet...even if I tried to get past someone unnoticed, they'd hear me coming from miles away. Also, I've been training my whole life with Blockhead, and I can proudly say I've gained more skills than I could've ever imagined. Everyone says I'm first in my class at swordsmanship...if I just go, all this would be in vain. That is, if they took me in anyway.'

'You have a point...' he murmured in response. 'I'd certainly go if I could, I've always dreamed of being a spy or an assassin, but thought it an impossible dream. What about you, Blake? would you rather stay or try this out?'

'I still don't know. I need more time to think about it.'

'Sure, you have plenty of time.'

'Right, it's not like if you go, I'll remain here on my own...' whispered Mark so only he could hear.

'Oh, I just realised though. Why would Jennifer want to go? Does she think she has the necessary natural skills to become a spy?' pointed out Blake all of a sudden, and as a result, Mark laughed.

'You make it so obvious you don't know her at all! She's the first person they'd accept. I remember when we were kids, back when Peter and I were her best and only friends, we used to come outside and play hide-and-seek. She was the best at it. No matter how much we searched for her, she kept changing her hiding place so we wouldn't find her, and did that in perfect silence, and fast too! Even when she sneaked right behind us, we'd have no clue she was there, so she always managed to scare us, or surprise us nevertheless. Even these days, whenever Peter and I would go looking for her, we would never find her unless she wanted us to. I don't know how she does it, but she does, and I think it's amazing. I always had this feeling she was watching us, probably laughing at us too, but as much as I looked around, I would never see her. Right now, I get the same feeling, that she's watching...' His words made the other two boys look behind in suspicion, but of course there was no sight of the girl.

'I guess that makes her a natural...' added Caliban after Mark fell silent, but then he started talking once more

'And because of it she'll have a great time, she'll be happy, and I'll be here, happy for her. Now if you'll excuse me...' he managed to whisper before leaving for his room as quickly as he could, before he loosened his grip on those rebel tears.

Once he was out of earshot, Blake told Caliban:

'I feel sorry for him…I really wish there was something we could do to help him.'

'Me too, but this is starting to become a personal matter... only they can solve it, and I sure hope they do.'

***

The boy was right; Jennifer had been watching the whole time. Sometimes she was just blushing, other times she was sad or disappointed in herself for the decision she was taking.

As soon as she noticed Mark leaving the group, she rushed

after him as quickly as she could manage with her wounds. The faster she moved, the worse her injuries would get, but she didn't care if her wounds were opening again. This was important.

Eventually, she managed to catch up with him right before he entered his room.

'Mark, wait!' she shouted, trying to hide the agony that was taking over as much on the outside as on the inside. The boy turned around with a very surprised look on his face, as if he was hearing a ghost of someone he had already lost.

'Jen? Jen, is that you?'

'Last I checked, yes.' They both smiled, but Mark had tears in his eyes. He was so excited he rushed over to hug her. 'Take it easy,' she protested. 'My wounds are open from running...ow!'

'Oops, I'm very sorry. Let me take you to the infirmary,' he said and raised her up to hold her.

'Thanks, but I'm fine.'

'I'm still taking you there, and I'm not letting you out of my sights anymore, you hear me?' he said, so she smiled.

'Good thing, because I meant to talk to you...and apologise for everything.'

'There's nothing you need to apologise for. Not to me, never apologise to me. Whatever you're doing, right or wrong, you have your reasons and I respect that.' She weakly smiled.

'I still have to explain everything.'

'Take your time, I'm listening,' he said faking a smile as he walked her to the infirmary.

23

Awesome Pictures

Late that afternoon, Mark was keeping Jennifer company in the infirmary, despite her protests that she was fine and could leave the place already. By that time, the girl explained what had happened, and apologised once more for her immature behaviour and for the decision she was taking.

'No, I told you, no apologising. I may not like it, but it's a great opportunity for you, and I don't want to be the reason you're stuck in one place against your will. I know you'll have a great time there, and that's all I could ask for. Those people will love you, I'm certain.'

'I wish you were coming too...'

'But I'm not,' he quickly said.

'Why not? I asked Blockhead, and he said that anyone can come.'

'It's not that. I'd love to come, but I'm thinking of the

consequences.'

'What are you talking about, Mark?' she asked with a hint of disappointment in her surprised tone.

'For a spy, you need to be quiet, quick to move and to think. I may be quick enough, but I'm definitely not silent. And besides, all my swordsmanship training would be in vain, and you very well know how far I have got.'

'I wish you weren't right,' she sighed.

'And on the other hand,' he continued, 'you have all of those skills. Like Caliban said, you're a natural.' She blushed, but didn't dare say anything. Soon, he continued anyway. 'Speaking of which, he said he wants to come to the Spy Headquarters too. You may not have my company there, but you'll have his, and I know he'll take good care of you.' He smiled, a very weak, but honest smile.

'I still wish it were you, though,' she whispered.

'Me too,' he sighed. 'Oh well,' he said louder, and livelier. 'This only means we have to make the best of the time remaining. That is, if you don't want to practice your spy skills anymore and vanish out of sight,' he winked, so she giggled.

'I guess I have plenty of time for that afterwards,' she said happily.

For a while, neither of them spoke. A doctor soon came and saw to the girl's wounds again. Jennifer even fell asleep, but Mark was always watching, careful not to fall asleep again. Fortunately, he didn't. Soon the girl woke up and asked what the time was.

'I have no idea. Give me a second, I'll go ask someone,' he said and left. A minute later he was back with the news. It was almost midnight, so she gasped.

'When did time fly by so quickly?'

'I have no idea, but we'd better take you to your room. I'm sure it's more comfortable than this place,' he smiled, and went to raise her up until she protested.

'I can walk, no need to force yourself to carry me. I only need a little support.'

He nodded and let her put an arm behind his neck and helped her to her room. The whole way, she did her best not to show she was limping, and hid the pain from her badly wounded abdomen.

'Are you sure you're alright?' he asked halfway, concerned that she was moving slower and slower.

'I'm fine, don't worry.'

Eventually they reached their destination. Before he let her go inside, Mark kissed her good night on the forehead, which made her let out a very big smile. Right before closing the door, the girl whispered:

'Don't stay up all night watching, okay? Get some sleep.' Then she closed the door and didn't see him until morning.

Despite her request, the boy couldn't help himself but keep watch for a bit. After an hour, he finally went to get some rest.

After getting several hours of sleep, Mark heard some powerful knocking at the door which woke him up. When he went to see who it was, he found none other than Caliban and Blake who were eager to find out all that happened the previous day when they weren't around. Apparently, they somehow found out that he spent some time with Jennifer.

'Fine, I'll tell you guys everything, just let me get changed first.'

The two boys nodded and waited outside. As soon as Mark came out, he started telling them everything as they were walking towards Jennifer's room to pick her up for breakfast. Caliban and Blake, who were supposed to just listen, continuously interrupted Mark's storytelling; usually with interjections like 'awe', 'that's nice' or 'hurrah'. It took longer to finish the story, especially since they kept asking for more details even after they reached the girl's room.

Eventually, they stopped, and knocked at the door waiting for the girl's response.

To their astonishment, as soon as they finished knocking the door opened, and there stood a cheerful Jennifer, ready for breakfast. When she saw their shocked expressions, she even started giggling.

'Good morning,' she told them.

'Good morning,' answered Mark. 'How are you feeling today, Jen?'

'Full of energy! I would've gone for some running today if not for my wounds.'

'Good to hear. Ready for breakfast?'

'I'm starving, let's go already,' cut in Blake all of a sudden.

'Me too,' added Caliban.

'Me three,' joked the girl.

'Me four,' finished Mark, and they all burst out laughing.

On the way, the four of them continued talking joyfully, joking and laughing as if they had no distress on their minds at all. The girl was finally healed on the inside, or so she let it show. However, once they got their food, silence took over for a while until the end of their meal.

Since she was first to finish eating, Jennifer broke the ice.

'So, when are you getting out of training? I heard you're training less this week.'

A few moments later, Blake swallowed his mouthful and answered.

'Just a couple of hours, by noon we should be out of there, and then we'll definitely spend some time with you, mademoiselle. Just tell us where to find you.'

'Well, I'm not exactly sure yet...I thought of checking the Warband Library.'

'We have a library?' asked Caliban astonished, but slightly disgusted by the thought of plain old boring paper.

'Apparently. I heard it's somewhere close to the garden entrance. It's probably that small old building we always passed by when going outside, remember? The one we thought might be haunted.' With their mouths full, the three boys nodded.

'Why do you want to go there though?' suddenly asked Mark right after having finished a glass of water.

'I just wanted to check if there's anything related to spies. I don't want to leave unprepared at all.'

'Oh! If you find anything with pictures let me know!' exclaimed Caliban all of a sudden.

'I'll keep an eye open,' she giggled. 'Anyway, with this occasion I'm discovering new places around the Warband Academy. Amazing, right? I never thought there was a place around that I didn't know about.'

'I doubt many people know we have a library at all.'

'I only found out from Blockhead yesterday when I asked

for his permission...he suggested I check the library first. I probably won't find much though, so if I leave that place before you guys get there, I'll most probably enjoy the nice weather outside.'

'Very well then,' said Mark. 'We should probably go to training now since we're all done eating. See you Jen afterwards, and be careful not to run or who knows what, okay?'

'Sure, I'll take care,' she promised.

***

The three boys went to training as usual, warm-up, training in swordsmanship and brawling, weight lifting and knife throwing. However, today Blockhead made a short announcement, saying that a new part of the Training Hall was open to young trainees: archery. He said it was necessary for each and every one of them to possess the archery skill, whether they will use it or not.

Most seemed pleased with the idea, some eager to be the first ones to give it a shot, but others wishing they weren't obliged to try it. Concerning the three boys, they didn't know what to expect, but out of them, Caliban seemed most excited.

'What an interesting way to finish our training for today! Let's try this and then go find Jennifer,' he said as he went towards the brand-new part of the Training Hall. Mark and Blake just followed without a word.

For half an hour they all practiced drawing the bow and hitting the targets, which was more exhausting for their arms than expected. The pressure on their fingertips quickly grew into pain. None of them managed to hit the targets, not even once. Blockhead encouraged everyone, telling them what they were doing wrong so they could fix it, and every now and then showing how himself. All of his advice helped them very much, and although the three boys missed the target, they were getting closer and closer, controlling the bow better each time.

After a while, they quit training for the day eager to find Jennifer and tell her all about it. Minutes later they were searching for the Warband Library. When they reached the building which the girl told them about.

'Are you sure this is it? It looks...abandoned,' Blake asked.

'We might as well go in and check,' answered Mark, uncertain himself.

And so, the boys opened the creaking entrance door and went in, a little frightened because of the spooky look of the place. As soon as they were all inside, an old man appeared behind them noisily shutting the door and greeted them. He might as well have been a ghost, or a risen undead by the looks of him.

'Hello, sir. Are you the library master?' asked Mark in doubt.

'If it's 'the librarian' you mean, then yes, that's me. I expect you're looking for the girl?' he asked, raising a bushy grey eyebrow. In response, the boys only nodded. 'Of course you didn't come for books. Well then, she only left minutes ago with three books. Wonderful girl that is, at least *someone* comes here for the sake of reading.' The old man stopped talking for a moment and continued with a soft thoughtful humming as he went on scratching his nearly bald head. 'Now where did she say she was going? *Hmmm...*'

'Maybe,' continued Caliban, 'somewhere out...'

'Outside!' the old man cut him off. 'To the gardens somewhere... I don't know, just go find her.' And with those words, the man kicked them out of the hostile looking building. Even though the boys' faces only showed surprise, they were actually glad they got out of there so quickly.

Their next destination was unclear, so they just went outside and searched everywhere. Only a couple of minutes later they found the girl lying on the grass under the shadow of a tree, with a book in her hands. Another two books were thrown next to her.

'Jen!' shouted Mark as the three of them went towards her. 'I see you got some books. I suppose you found what you were looking for.'

'You have no idea,' she said excitedly. 'Look,' she said as soon as the boys were down on the grass too. The four of them made a circle, with the books in the middle. 'These two seem to be novels. Now I was reading this one, entitled *Invisible or in the Shadows*. It's about a young boy who one day saw a man lurking in the shadows, but whom no other person seemed to notice. The man was a master spy, and when he found out the young boy had the skill to detect him, he made him his trainee. That's as far as I reached in the story, but it definitely seems interesting!' she said, and then looked at Caliban and continued. 'Sorry Cal, it doesn't have pictures,' she apologised and he laughed.

'Don't worry, I'll try reading it nevertheless, especially since you say it's so interesting. So, what about the third book, the one that's not a novel?'

'Right. Well, this one *does* have some pictures, but that's because it's a beginner's guide to spying.'

'What's it called? Does it have an awesome name like that novel?'

'It's called *A Beginner's Guide to Spying*,' she said, which made Caliban let out an *oh*, and the others burst out in laughter.

'Well, don't just sit there, let me see it!' he exclaimed excitedly, so the girl handed him the book. 'Introduction, blah blah blah, 'this book contains the basic of everything you need to know', let's skip this. Oh! Just look at that!' he suddenly shouted out, and showed each of them some pictures with some men in strange poses. 'Is it just me, or are these fighting moves? Look, there's a low kick, a high kick, a back kick, a twist and a turn but no crude punches like the ones in our brawling sessions. Oh my god this is so interesting!'

'If you spend a moment to read the description below, you'll see this is not brawling, it's some sort of martial arts. Even a spy needs to know some fighting skills apparently, but he cannot take with him more than an assassination dagger and his own body, because fighting accessories usually make sounds, revealing the location of the spy.'

'This is fascinating, Jen,' said Mark. 'You certainly seem to like talking about this,' he smiled and then asked: 'When did you have time to read all that? That crazy library master said you only left minutes before we got there.'

'Indeed, the crazy *librarian* was saying the truth. I didn't read everything there, just checked a couple of pictures and read in between the lines. Then I started reading the novel and you showed up.'

'You sure are quick in everything,' he said, a little surprised. 'Anyway, we wanted to tell you something about training today.' The girl raised an eyebrow.

'Oui. It's something really interesting,' cut in Blake. 'Blockhead introduced archery!'

'Archery!' she exclaimed surprised. 'But that's one of the very few things a spy is allowed to carry: a bow and arrows. That doesn't involve much movement, does it?' she asked and the boys approved. *This can't be a coincidence,* she thought to herself, and Blurreydal agreed. 'Tomorrow I'm coming with you to the Training Halls,' she declared, but the boys tried to protest. 'But you agreed that it doesn't involve much moving, so why couldn't I do it?'

After a few minutes of protests and complaints, the boys gave up when they realised there was no talking her out of it. Besides, she was right too! There was no reason she couldn't do it.

'It's settled then!' she said smiling.

24

Plan, Sweet Plan

Later the same afternoon, the three boys and the girl remembered they had an important plan to put into practice.

Mark first explained that he managed to get that H4K from Nico, so now they could record that message they meant to share with the leaders. As soon as he finished his short storytelling, Jennifer burst out in excitement, hugging each and one of them before apologising for the awkward moment. In return, the boys just laughed in amusement.

'Well then, where should we record the message?' asked the girl, suddenly serious.

'The place doesn't matter so long as it's quiet and nobody hears us. There will be no image, so the environment is not important,' answered Mark. 'I have a feel we got the faulty prototype, but oh well!'

'Aw, but what about my glasses and wig and cool coat and all that?' cried out Caliban, which made them all laugh until their cheeks hurt.

'We're sorry, Cal,' eventually managed to say Jennifer in between breaths. 'Maybe next time.'

'Back to business,' joined in Blake. 'Where are we going to record that message?'

After a couple of minutes of thinking, the girl spoke out shyly:

'I was thinking that maybe we could in the library? It's the quietest place, and I'm sure the librarian won't mind.'

'And the creepiest place too,' pointed out Caliban. 'Maybe we could do it in one of our bedrooms? But if we do, don't let it be mine, it's all messed up!'

'There's going to be a lot of background noise from others walking, talking, maybe even screaming on the corridor. We'd have to try to record it lots of times before getting it right,' explained Jennifer. 'This is why I was thinking of the library, but if you guys have a better idea, I'd like to hear it. I don't like the library, nor the librarian, half as much as you do.'

'It would've been nice if we could just do it here, outside. Unfortunately, we're in public,' sighed Blake.

'Actually...' joined in Mark. 'I might know a place outside that we could use to record our message. It's that corner behind the Academy where nobody hangs out because it's gloomy and lifeless. There's nobody to hear us, and nobody we can hear.' The others seemed pleased by the suggestion, and Jennifer spoke out:

'Sounds like a plan then! Show us the way!'

Without wasting a single minute, Mark went ahead, leading the way, while Caliban and Blake helped Jennifer up and stayed with her to make sure she wasn't left behind. Several minutes later they reached their destination, and Blake said that it was the quietest place he had ever been to.

'Toooo...tooo...too...ooo!'

'What was that?' asked in astonishment Caliban, to which Blake explained that it was just his echo.

'This place is perfect!' exclaimed Jennifer, which made Mark blush for a second. 'The echo is going to make our voices sound a little different, and there will be a controlled background noise to make it sound...well, alien and official maybe?' The boys giggled, and so did their echo for another few seconds. 'Alright, who is going to talk? It can't be me because my voice is much softer, so they're going to catch me right away.'

'Can it still be me?' asked Caliban, anxious.

'Alright then. Do you know what you're supposed to say?' The boy nodded, took a few breaths and asked Mark to start the recording. Without any comment, he started the recording, and made a sign for the others to keep quiet.

With a deeper, faked voice, Caliban started talking, very dramatically:

'Hello gentlemen! You are probably wondering who I am and why I am sending this recording. I am sorry to notify you that only the latter shall be explained. You must surely know that the human race is at war with the alien race. By sending you this message, my goal is to help you think twice about the matter at hand, and to make sure the war comes to an end, on peaceful terms. I am asking you to listen to me, and think of the reason that made this war start in the first place. Was it you who made the first move, or was it the aliens attacking you without reason?'

Caliban took a deep breath before continuing, letting the echo do its job and create the needed atmosphere. The others did their best to restrain themselves from laughing.

'Now that you have hopefully thought about the matter, I need to inform you that the alien race has recently helped several of your Academy trainees in need, by resurrecting them from the lands of the dead. Yes indeed, you have heard me right; the aliens revived your soldiers, the soldiers you are using against them, in order to show that they mean no harm, and never wanted this war to take place.' The boy took another deep breath and let out a little sigh of relief. 'Thank you for listening, gentlemen.'

As soon as Mark stopped the recording, Jennifer burst out happily, saying: 'That was perfect! This will definitely make them realise the mistake they're making. And nice voice change by the way, Cal!'

The boy laughed, and using that grave voice again, he thanked her, making them all laugh. As soon as they all calmed down, Blake said:

'Now that we've got that out of the way, there's just one more thing we have to do before we're officially done, and that's getting our leaders to hear the recording. The question is how.'

'We got this far; we're not going to give up now! One way or another we're going to do it!' confidently said Caliban.

'I might have an idea,' started Blake. 'But I don't think it's great though…' The others listened curiously. 'I'm guessing that before they are used, these devices are first tested, and that will bring up the recorded message if there is one. Maybe if we bring it back to the lab, the scientists will test it at some point and hear our recording, and bring it to the leaders themselves.'

'It could work…but we can't take chances now,' said Jennifer. 'What if they decide to delete the message instead? Luckily, I have another idea. Cal and I are going to be trainee spies soon, so we might as well start our training by sneaking into their office when they're not there and leave the H4K.'

'That's too risky,' joined in Mark. 'You, Jen, are not healed yet, so you can't do it, and even if Caliban goes, they're bound to have traps and alarms set in there, so I doubt you could get in without notice.'

'First of all, we could wait a couple of days for me to heal, we're not in that much of a hurry! And second, if you have a better idea, I'd like to hear it.'

'Um, well…it's not the greatest of ideas, and it might sound really strange, but I was thinking that maybe Blockhead could help us. I'm starting to trust him lately.' Blake, Caliban and Jennifer's eyes went wide open in shock.

'I'm starting to trust him too, but not that much,' she replied. 'He's one of them, you know that. There's no way he is going to help us. We can't risk it!'

'You're saying it as if your idea wasn't risky. At least my idea doesn't involve any of us being at risk by breaking the rules. If he doesn't help us, we'll just find another way.'

'And then we'll have to double risk it, right? If he doesn't help us, he's bound to warn the leaders of what we're trying to do, and then there's no way we're getting our message through, especially not undetected.'

'Guys, stop arguing, it's getting us nowhere!' shouted Caliban, leaving Mark and Jennifer in total silence. 'I say we vote.' They all seemed to agree. 'I vote for Blake's plan, and Smotch says he votes for Jennifer's.'

'Well, I vote for my own plan,' the girl said. 'And Blur the same.'

'I vote for my own plan too,' said Mark, furiously looking at the girl.

'Sange and I vote for Mark's plan,' said Blake.

'Ha! I win!' shouted the boy, but then Jennifer stopped him.

'No, you didn't, it's a tie between us. We have three votes each. This means Caliban has to pick again.'

Hearing those words made Caliban feel tense all of a sudden. 'I have to take sides?' The others nodded. 'Fine...' he sighed. 'I pick...' he slowly said, looking at each of them in turns. 'I pick Jennifer's plan,' he said, and then whispered, 'sorry Mark,' just as he was letting out a *humph* in frustration, or maybe disappointment? Either way, Jennifer was the winner, so they would put her plan into practice.

'Well then, I guess we still have a couple of days to refine everything until I heal. I plan to go in action myself with Caliban. Two heads are always better than one.'

'That's right,' said Mark as he rolled his eyes. 'Leave me and Blake behind. It's not as if we could help to, no...'

'Mark,' started answering the girl. 'You should be happy you don't need to do anything anymore. I think Cal and I can handle it from here, but if we do need help with something, we'll certainly ask you two.'

'She's right, Mark, deal with it,' added Caliban.

'And suddenly you're on her side, no matter what I say or do, huh?' he ended up saying and left in a hurry.

'Should we follow him?' asked Blake, a little disturbed by the boy's reaction.

'He's fine,' answered Jennifer. 'He just doesn't like to lose. What do you think made him such a great swordsman? All he needs right now is a little time alone.'

'If you say so...' said Blake, not sure if she was right or not. 'I think he's also a bit jealous.'

'Jealous! What makes you think he might be jealous?'

'Well...I'm pretty sure you noticed yourself, but I'm still going to say it.' Before continuing, Blake took a peek behind to check if Mark was still there, eavesdropping, but apparently it was all clear, so he went on. 'That boy likes you a lot, and enjoys spending time with you, but this hasn't happened much lately, and now that he knows you'll soon be leaving without him being able to come as well is breaking him apart piece by piece. The fact that you won the vote because of Caliban made him snap.'

'So...what you're saying is that he's jealous of Cal?' The girl looked at Caliban who only shrugged back at her saying:

'Don't look at me, I'm not doing this on purpose!'

'So, what am I supposed to do in this case?' she looked at Blake in desperation.

'I'm guessing he expected you to go after him when he left, but it's too late for that now, so that leaves you with nothing you can do about it.' The girl sighed.

'I suppose this is the price to pay for being the only girl around,' said Caliban, trying to make it sound like a joke, but instead it made the girl let out another even bigger sigh.

'Then I don't like being *the* girl. I wish being a girl in this world was just as ordinary as being a boy.' The girl sighed again and stood up, holding her three new books. 'Let's just call it a day and go to sleep. It's going to get dark in an hour or so.' The boys watched her get up, and opened their mouths to offer her help with walking, but she quickly dismissed them by saying, 'And I need no help to walk, I'm fine, just slow.'

'Very well then,' said Caliban. 'We'll stay here a while longer, see you tomorrow at breakfast.' They all waved goodbye.

For a minute the two boys stood in silence, waiting for the girl to get out of earshot. As soon as she was far enough, Caliban started:

'I feel so stupid right now!' and he hit his forehead with the palm of his hand. 'I wish she wasn't *the* girl just as much as she does.'

'Hey, it's not your fault she is.'

'But it's my fault for ending up spending so much time with her. If I hadn't, Mark wouldn't be so annoyed right now. His problem is me, and you know it.'

'Yes, most probably, but you can't control his jealousy, you should know that. And anyway, it's normal to have feelings for someone,' he winked.

'But I don't like her in the same way that Mark does, and I don't plan to either. It's appearances that makes you guys think so.'

'Smotch doesn't seem to agree,' said Blake, point out the

heart-shaped tattoo on Caliban's neck that Smolther was forming.

'Fine, maybe I do like her in that way, but I never planned to. I know her place is with Mark, not me. By the way, how bad do you think he hates me right now?'

'Probably bad enough to place an arrow through your skull...' Caliban gulped. 'But you never know. Mark's very unpredictable, he might be perfectly fine in the morning,' said Blake.

'How reassuring...' sarcastically said Caliban. 'It's starting to get dark, we'd better get in,' he said, to which the other boy agreed and they went to sleep.

25

Betrayal

The following morning, the boys met up for breakfast, and expected the girl to join them too, but she was nowhere to be seen in the cafeteria. Meanwhile, Mark and Caliban didn't dare lock eyes, and Blake was afraid to say anything so they wouldn't get even more upset.

After a while of tense silence, they eventually went directly to the Training Room. To their surprise, Jennifer was already there, practicing her archery skills. She seemed a natural.

Before they managed to go up to her to ask why she didn't show up for breakfast, Blockhead stopped them in order to remind them that soon they would be back to the normal training program, no excuses. In response, they let out a big sigh in unison, and quickly left to talk with Jennifer, who saw them coming.

'Good morning, boys, how are you?'

'We're all good,' said Blake, taking a peek at the other two boys just to see them looking in opposite directions. They refused to look the other in the eye. 'Jennifer, why didn't you come for breakfast? We were starting to get worried.'

'Sorry, I just didn't feel hungry because I was so excited to try the archery thing you told me about. No need to get worried about me all the time, you know!' she said with a little smile.

'You seem good at it. Did you do this before?' continued Blake. The other two wouldn't say a thing.

'Actually, it's my first time. It's really easy. Blockhead taught me the basics earlier when I got here, and since then I've been practicing. Come, I'll show you.'

'Thanks, but I'm not so eager to master my archery skills. How about you teach these two freaks here, I'm sure they'll be more interested,' he said as he put his hands around each of their necks, bringing them a little closer. The first to say anything was Mark.

'To be honest, I don't really like archery,' he said, and then Caliban spoke out too.

'You mentioned archery is important for spies to know, right? I'm interested then.'

'Me too!' suddenly said Mark, which made Jennifer raise an eyebrow. She didn't say more than a simple 'OK' and went straight to the point; explaining how it's done and showing them the movement.

Jennifer wasn't a great archer yet, and never managed to hit the bull's eye, but seemed to be an excellent teacher, because the boys quickly started to hit the target themselves. She showed them how to draw the bow and how to keep the arrow fixed in order to control its destination. She always reminded them not to forget to breathe deeply and calmly before every shot, and most importantly, to focus each time and not rush.

'Imagine you're a sniper,' she tried to explain. 'Unless the conditions, the wind and the target, are just as you need them to be, you're not taking the shot. Same with archery. In our case it's easy, because there's no wind inside, and the targets aren't moving, but you still have to focus just as much.'

The girl admitted that her explanations weren't even close to perfect, but she still seemed to make the boys understand how they're supposed to use the bow and arrow, she even made Blake intrigued.

Before they knew it, several hours had already passed by, and they had made a lot of progress. Their arms and fingertips burned with pain and exhaustion. When they finally took a real break, Blockhead went over to congratulate them, especially Jennifer.

'I will be honest with you, kids,' he then said. 'The real reason for which I included archery in the Training Room is because the Headmasters at the Spy Headquarters asked me to. Each spy of theirs is experienced in archery, and I wanted you to be as well, especially if you go there...just to make things easier,' he said with a wink. 'First I thought that I would take it away after you have gone, but it seems to have quite some success, so I suppose I'll leave it for a while longer for those staying.'

'Thank you, sir,' said Jennifer. 'I'm very glad to have tried archery, and more excited that I will practice it more often soon.'

'I dare say the same, sir,' added Caliban. 'If not for our practice here, things could have been extremely tough after we left. I must thank you deeply,' and he bowed, which made the girl giggle and Mark mutter a *humph* in frustration. Blake showed no particular reaction.

'I'll leave you to it, then,' finished Blockhead and he went in the opposite direction.

Not even a minute later, Mark asked the girl if there was anything besides archery that she wanted to do, but she was out of ideas. However, Blake came up with an idea.

'How about us boys have a duel and you watch and give us advice? I don't think it's a great idea for you to get involved in a fight yourself just yet. And besides, you seem to be a great teacher,' he explained, and the girl nodded in agreement.

'Sounds like a plan. So, who goes first? Any offers?'

For a minute they were silent, but then one of them broke the silence with an unnaturally low mysterious voice.

'I want to be first.' It was Mark talking. 'Caliban, I challenge you,' he said turning to him, a wide smile on his face and mischief in his eyes. With a moment of hesitation, the challenge was accepted and they grabbed their swords.

'Alright,' started Jennifer, 'remember, when I tell you to stop, you freeze in place so I can tell or show you something regarding that position.' The boys nodded. 'Three, two, one... start!'

Without hesitation, Mark rushed for the first strike, and Caliban barely had time to dodge. He was already off balance. Mark went for a quick second strike, but Caliban parried and threw Mark off balance in the process.

'He's strong,' he whispered under his breath before charging for his first hit, but before he managed to finish his move, Jennifer shouted 'stop' so he froze in place as asked to, the blade in midair. Mark had gained back his balance and was ready to block, but was startled at the sound and stopped too. He looked at the approaching girl in confusion.

'Cal, you're holding your sword wrong. With that movement you'll gain no speed and your hit will be easily blocked, with or without good reflexes. And Mark, you should try focusing on your guard. You're not stable enough,' she said as she pushed his right leg from behind which made him fall to the ground. 'Bend your knees more, and tense those muscles so that nothing can move you. Also, your feet are too close, if I push you, you'll immediately lose your balance. This is available for you too, Cal.' The girl turned back to her watching place and told them to start over.

This time she didn't stop them for a much longer time. They kept exchanging blows until Caliban felt weak, so weak that his body started shivering when he tried to tense his muscles. On the other hand, Mark seemed full of energy, with a bloodthirsty look in his eyes. As a consequence, he took advantage of his opponent's instability and did his *coup de grace* using all his force. As he expected, Caliban tried to block, but the force overwhelmed him, so he fell on his back with a loud *thud* which sent shivers through Jennifer.

Immediately she approached them shouting 'Enough!' However, Mark didn't stop until he pointed the tip of his sword to Caliban's chest. The girl seemed worried.

Without another word, she placed herself in between a defeated Caliban and a proud Mark. Jennifer helped the fallen boy back to his feet.

'Ow! My back! That was one nasty fall,' moaned the victim. For some reason, Mark seemed happy to see Caliban in agony.

'This was supposed to be just some practice...' whispered Jennifer in sympathy. 'Let's take you to the infirmary, Cal,' she added as she helped him on his feet, putting his hand around her shoulders for stability. As they started moving towards the exit, she glanced at Mark for just a second with an obvious frown on her face. He stopped smiling all of a sudden and opened his mouth to say something, but changed his mind and let her go with the hurt boy.

After a few steps, Jennifer kindly said: 'Cal, you have to learn how to fall without hurting yourself. We'll focus on that tomorrow if you're feeling well.' The boy only nodded, too weakened to even talk, and moved by the fact that the girl cared so much. He wondered why.

Back at the duelling circle, Mark and Blake stood staring at each other in silence. Blake was too shocked to make a move or react to anything. He knew it was his stupid idea that caused this whole problem.

Mark stared at him in confusion, until he eventually broke the silence.

'That's not what I meant to happen...'

At the sound of his talking, Blake snapped out of his daydreaming, and quickly added in a whisper, 'it's my fault.'

'Don't take the blame. It's all my fault and you know it. I was just angry...I wanted to show Jen I'm better than him, and I wanted him to hurt... but I never meant for it to go that far. She probably thinks I'm a monster,' he sighed and threw himself on the floor, his hands covering his face and he started shouting. 'Nothing is going as it should!'

Blake didn't know what to do or say to comfort him, so he just tried changing the subject, although he knew it would be in vain. Still, Mark was eager to get his mind off the subject so he accepted Blake's offer to do something else.

****

At the infirmary, Caliban was cared for while Jennifer waited outside his ward. After a while she went in to check on him, only to see his puzzled face.

'I didn't expect you to still be here.'

'I can't leave without knowing you'll be fine. So how are you feeling?' she asked in sympathy.

'Much better now, thanks for caring, that's really sweet of you,' he said, which made the girl blush a little. 'The doctor said that I have nothing broken and it's no serious injury, so if I sit and rest until tomorrow, I'll be as good as new.'

'That's wonderful news!' she exclaimed.

The boy closed his eyes in order to relax and for a minute they didn't talk. When he opened them back, he realised that the girl hadn't left, and was actually sitting on a chair next to him.

'You don't have to stay if you don't want to, Jennifer,' he said, trying to sound strong, but in his voice, weakness could be heard.

'Of course I have to! It's the least I can do. Keep in mind that I didn't stop the duel in time. And besides, you need some company. I know how lonely one can get in these rooms,' she said, watching the ceiling, searching for the brown spots of age she knew so well. They were still there.

In the meantime, the blue bracelet on her hand transformed into the tiny human-like Blurreydal. Noticing, Smolther did the same, but not after taking a heart shaped tattoo for just a second. Only the blue alien seemed to notice.

'Looks like they're sitting comfy, them two,' said the boy with a faint smile as he watched the little aliens.

'Black and blue definitely go great together,' noticed the girl, but she then swallowed her words, wishing she had never said them out loud. She changed the subject.

For a while, they went on talking about nothing in particular. Before they knew it, they both fell asleep. The girl never moved from the chair until she made sure the boy was asleep. Then she let herself lower her head on the little table next to the bed and closed her eyes.

About an hour later, the door slowly cracked open without waking either of the sleeping people. A head popped in through the opening, inspecting what was inside.

Mark had come to apologise to Caliban, but when he saw Jennifer in there too, sleeping deeply, his breath was taken away, and his throat was burning.

Without a second thought, he closed back the door and pushed himself against the wall in confusion and in deep thought.

Jennifer had stayed with Caliban that whole time, and even

fell asleep while keeping him company...just like he did when she was in the infirmary ward. She couldn't...right?

26

Judgement

The following morning, the four friends met in the training hall. Mark and Blake had breakfast together, just like Jennifer and Caliban did.

When he woke up in the infirmary ward, Caliban was astonished, but also relieved to see the girl still in the room, although she was still fast asleep. *She's adorable when she's sleeping.*

He was feeling much better in comparison to the previous day, so he decided to pick her up and take her for breakfast. She would wake up on the way eventually, he was sure.

His hypothesis proved to be right as soon as they reached their destination. All faces were turned to look at them, but he gave them no attention. However, when the girl woke up, she was very confused to find herself in someone's arms in the cafeteria while all eyes were on her. At least Mark wasn't there at the time, so he wouldn't find out to make matters worse.

When she looked up at the man holding her, she awkwardly said, 'Morning, Cal.' With only a faint smile he let her down. 'I didn't expect to wake up like this...'

'Sorry, but I couldn't waste any time. We've got a long and full day ahead. You need to teach me how to fall, remember?'

'That's right,' she answered, unable to control the blush that was coming. 'I'm famished, let's eat,' she quickly added in an attempt to change the subject. Without a comment they started eating and then went to the Training Hall where they met with the other two boys.

The first thing they stumbled upon was Mark's apologies for the previous day. He didn't mention that he saw them both in the infirmary ward, and Blake didn't know about it either. It was his little secret.

As soon as he was done apologising, the girl changed the subject. 'I'm going to teach Cal how to fall without getting hurt, so if you don't have anything better to do, you two should come too,' she invited them.

'That would be nice,' agreed both of them.

'Ok, let's go and warm-up first and then stay in that area. The floor is softer in that part of the Hall which will make it safer.' The boys nodded and followed her lead. As soon as they warmed up, the girl explained what 'knowing how to fall' meant, because they didn't believe you needed any skill to be able to fall.

'This is about falling right, without harming yourself. It can be very painful as you well know,' she mentioned, to which Caliban nodded, 'So it's important to know how to fall right.

First of all, you keep your backbone safe. For example, when you fall with your face down, you have to touch the floor with your palms and elbows at the same time, forming a triangle with your big and index fingers. The vertebral column has to be straight, and the abdominal muscles tense. Your head must be turned to the side so you don't end up falling on your face by accident. For balance, don't keep your feet too close. Just like this.'

While the boys had very confused looks on their faces, she tried to show them exactly what she was talking about, so she threw herself forward, respecting all the details she mentioned a minute earlier.

'That looks painful,' commented Caliban, remembering his own pain from the previous day.

'But if done right, it's not. I'm perfectly fine as you can see.'

'When did you learn this?' questioned Mark, very curious.

'I remember Blockhead showed me how to do this when I was about ten or so. He once saw me climb every tree outside and worried I might fall and get hurt. That was way before the daily training program. I may be out of practice now, but I still remember what he taught me.' She smiled widely and asked them to stop changing the subject and try to do it themselves.

Leaving them to try over and over again until their elbows hurt, the girl continued her lesson.

'Next is falling on your back. The secret is not to stop once you hit the floor, but continue the movement for a while longer, and let the pressure go to the scapula,' she told them, motioning toward behind her shoulders. 'Push me, I'll show you,' she then added so they started at her in wonder. 'Come on, don't be chickens,' she mocked them when they wouldn't react. Eventually Blake pushed her shoulder back and she fell to the floor. Unlike the boys expected, once she hit the floor, the movement wasn't over, just like she said. Without any apparent effort she stood back up and encouraged them to try too.

They continued their falling training for another half hour and until they realised their backs were numb. However, they were grateful for Jennifer's great teaching and thanked her. Their backbones were completely intact; it was just the muscles that were a bit sore.

From a distance, Blockhead had been watching them for a while. In his mind flashed memories since the girl was just a child, and sadness took over. Still, he was proud of her, just like any parent would be.

Training seemed to pass by quickly for the four kids. Except Mark of course. Being around Caliban was no less annoying than the previous day, but this time he managed to hold in his negative feelings. He talked little, if at all, in fear of saying something offensive. Jennifer noticed, with Blurreydal's help of course, but decided against bringing up the subject. She'd find a time to discuss it with Blake and understand exactly what's going on.

As soon as they went out of the Training Hall, the girl asked what they should do. Finally, they decided to go outside to that quiet place and talk about the plan to implant the message they recorded.

'We're running out of time and we need to get them to listen to the recording before we leave,' said Jennifer, making sure not to mention Caliban's name in any context.

'I don't see how this plan is supposed to work in the first place,' said Mark in a grumpy tone, and refused to help.

He could leave in this case, said Blurreydal.

I wonder why he's still staying. There must be a reason... Jennifer added in her mind so that just the blue alien would hear.

'Theoretically speaking,' started saying Caliban, 'we have to know when they go out of their office, so I suppose we have to spy on them a little so as to understand their routine. See when they go out and back in and so on.'

'Actually,' interrupted Blake, 'that won't be necessary.' Even Mark raised an eyebrow in astonishment. Seeing their shocked faces, the boy continued. 'I grew up in there, I know all these things...just like Jennifer learned the falling techniques with Blockhead. They took me in when I was little because they saw me as a quiet and thoughtful child, and thought I'd have a great future in politics. I used to spend more time in there than we do now in training.'

The three listening didn't dare say a word or ask anything, so they waited for Blake to continue speaking. Eventually, after a melancholic sigh, he did.

'Trying to go there during the day is pointless. There's at least one person inside during the day and there is high-tech security active during the night. Also, they open only to fingerprints, so there's no way you can get inside unless one of them lets you in. Also, need I mention that there are guards at the entrance all the time? No, you can't get in,' he shook his head.

'Ok, you're right, but we can't give up so easily,' said Jennifer, and the boys let out a faint smile seeing her excitement. 'One way or another we'll make them find the H4K. How about we leave it on the hallway overnight for them to see it in the morning?'

'I told you, there are guards guarding the door.'

'Who mentioned any door? We can leave it further away, somewhere out of their sight, but a noticeable place for those going there.'

'That might actually be a good and simple idea,' admitted Blake. 'So, who will do the job after all?'

'We already decided that Jennifer and I would go,' joined in Caliban. 'I think we should do it a day or two before we leave, just in case they decide to search for their intruders,' he winked. Mark didn't show any reaction, but watched every detail.

'Sounds like a plan,' she said, Blake nodded in agreement. Noticing Mark's expressionless face, she asked for his opinion.

'I'm sure your plan will go well,' he said, as dull as possible, as if he didn't care. A minute later he stood up and left without another word.

What's wrong with him? she asked herself.

I don't understand his feelings either. Maybe he feels left out. Maybe...

Taking her by surprise, Caliban stood up too. 'I'll go talk to him. See you later,' and he ran off trying to catch up with him, leaving Jennifer and Blake on their own.

The girl was mostly disappointed in the turn of events, but also grateful since she had a moment to talk with Blake in private. Before saying anything, she sighed, picking her words with care.

'Blake, why do you think they're acting like this lately?'

'We're talking about Mark and Cal here, right?' She just nodded. 'Well...to keep it simple, Mark is craving attention and is jealous, but you already know that.'

'What about Cal? He seems changed too...' she whispered, watching the ground and playing with her fingers.

'Um...I guess he's just confused like you and me?' The girl frowned. She wanted the real answer. Eventually he sighed and told her the truth. 'He feels the same as Mark does, but tries not to show it because he's ashamed and doesn't want to cause problems between you and Mark. But don't tell him I told you, he'd kill me!'

He is right, Jenif. You cannot let him know you know.

'Ok, I promise I won't confront him about it.'

Is that why he carried me up in the morning instead of waking me up? The thought confused her, so she tried to ignore it. What was done was done, she had to accept the facts.

The girl was so deep in her thoughts that she didn't even hear Blake telling her they should go find those two before they start another war.

'Jennifer!'

'Yes, sorry. I'm coming,' and she stood up, catching up with him.

***

Meanwhile, Caliban ran after Mark, managing to catch up with him. To his surprise, he wasn't trying to get away or avoid him, so they ended up facing each other on a main corridor where many trainees passed by.

'Mark!' called out Caliban. 'Slow down, please!'

'What do you want?' He seemed a little frustrated, so Caliban tried being as straightforward as possible.

'Why did you leave just now?'

'My part in the plan is over. There was no point in remaining there.'

'You could've at least said 'bye', but I know that's not the real answer. Just tell me the truth.' Caliban's eyes begged for an answer which seemed to never come. Instead of speaking out, Mark looked away from Caliban without moving. Eventually he gave a short and whispered answer:

'I can't bear to see you and Jen together, I just had to get away from it.'

'Mark, listen to me,' Caliban put a hand on his shoulder before continuing. 'There is nothing going on between me and your Jen.'

'Humph, so *you* say.'

'What do you mean?'

When answering, Mark looked at Caliban in the eyes.

'Cal, I saw you last night in the infirmary, I meant to apologise then, but then I saw Jen sleeping there too and I couldn't bear the sight. Don't you see? I'm losing her...' he looked away once more, and his next words were no more than a faint whisper. 'And there's nothing I can do about it.'

Caliban was speechless. Of all outcomes, this is the least he expected to happen, but he realised Mark was right. Jennifer really did spend less time with Mark and more time with him.

She made sure he would be fine when he was hurt, and they would both be going to the Spy Headquarters soon, leaving Mark behind.

Sorry, Smotch, now I realise what you tried to tell me.

'I didn't mean for it to be like this,' he looked down at his feet, ashamed of himself, not daring to look Mark in the eyes. By the time he raised his head to look forward, Mark had already turned his back and was walking away, soon blending into the crowd.

From behind he heard shouts coming from two different voices. 'Mark, Cal! Where are you?' It was obviously Jennifer and Blake.

This was the worst time to talk with either of them, so he ran to his room, disappearing in the crowd. He needed to talk with someone about everything that was happening, and that one was Smolther.

'I guess they're not here,' said the girl, disappointed, and Blake shrugged.

'If they do start a war, we'll surely hear about it.' The thought made Jennifer laugh. Of course they'd find out, at some point anyway.

27

Confusion

For the rest of the day, each of the young trainees remained alone in their rooms. Until falling asleep, Jennifer daydreamed, imagining how things would turn out alright, both on political and social levels. They seemed equally important now. Even Blurreydal understood her way of thinking.

The next morning, she woke up earlier than usual.

Without hesitation, she got ready and went for breakfast. The canteen was empty except for her, and it was only after she left, that others started arriving. Her friends were probably all still sleeping.

She went directly to the training hall, hoping to find Blockhead there. She couldn't understand why, but she felt like he was the one who was supposed to listen to the things she was going through. To her surprise, and relief, he was already there, doing his usual check-up on the equipment. Before the girl had time to tell him good morning, he had already heard her footsteps and spoke.

'What's with you up so early?'

'I...I don't really know.' It was true, she didn't know why she was there so early. The man turned to face her as she walked closer.

'It's barely six o'clock. I expected you to still be in bed. Did something happen?'

'You could say that, but I don't know how to explain.'

'You don't have to tell me if you don't want to, you know.' The girl remained silent. When Blockhead started turning back to resume his work, the girl spoke out, confessing her troubles.

'It's about Mark and Caliban. They're fighting over me and I don't know what to do.' She let it all out in a single breath, speaking quickly, and waited for a reaction.

At first, her trainer only turned to face her. Little by little, his facial muscles contracted in a strange way and he laughed. It was the strangest, and the scariest sound the girl had ever heard.

'It's not funny!' she complained, afraid that she had made a fool of herself. Why did she ever think that talking to Blockhead would make her feel any better? She felt so frustrated and turned on her heels, ready to leave. However, before having time to take a step, the man calmed down and put his hand on her shoulder so she'd stop moving.

'I'm sorry, it's not funny, you're right. I just found it hard to take in. Thing is, I expected this kind of thing to happen years ago, and since it didn't, I thought it never would. It just took me by surprise, that's all.'

The girl stared at him in wonder, trying to understand the meaning behind his words. She remained silent as he carried on talking.

'So, you say they're fighting over you? Do you mind giving me more details?' The girl bit her lip in hesitation, but answered nevertheless.

'Ever since I started spending time with Caliban, Mark has become jealous for some reason. He has been acting strange. I don't want to hurt either of them, or let them hurt each other again. I don't know what to do.'

'Jennifer, I'm no good in giving social advice, but I think that the best solution now is to talk with Mark. Since you're leaving soon, he probably wants to spend as much time with you as he can. It's natural.'

The girl looked down in shame. She already knew that was what she ought to do, but somehow it wasn't as simple as it seemed. She remained silent, so Blockhead attempted to change the subject.

'I really like your bracelet. The colour looks so *alive.*' The girl's heartbeat suddenly accelerated because she didn't want her trainer to know she had contact with those who were supposed to be the enemy. 'I have a grey boot knife,' he suddenly said out of the blue with a wink. He then turned back to his business, and left the girl on her own, staring into the void.

Then, something just clicked inside her head as she put his two apparently random sentences together.

Blur, are there aliens who can take the shape of a weapon?

Yes, Jenif.

The girl didn't know what to think, but she couldn't gather her thoughts so early in the morning and let it slip away. She had to discuss it with the boys anyway.

Seeing that she was alone, Jennifer went to practice her archery. What she didn't know was that Blockhead was constantly checking on her in the corner of the eye as he was doing his usual check-up routine before the place got crowded.

Her skill with the bow was getting better and better. Little by little, she became swifter and her accuracy increased each time. It felt so easy, and she loved the feel of the bow and arrow in her hands. She felt elegant for once.

At some point, maybe half an hour later, Blake showed up with Mark and greeted Jennifer as soon as they saw her. Deep down, she was glad that Caliban wasn't there too.

'Wow, Jennifer, you're so good with the bow already!' exclaimed Blake, and Mark nodded in approval. She blushed and thanked them.

'It's easy to learn something you're passionate about,' she told them.

'Then are you going to do this all day?' asked Mark. Whatever he wanted to hear was a mystery to the girl who answered, but he seemed pleased either way.

'Unless I find something else to do, then yes. Feel free to join me if you want.' Mark smiled at her words, and accepted the invitation. Blake joined in as well because he had nothing else to do on his own. Besides, everything else was much more tiring than archery, so little by little even he started to like it.

They lost track of time, enjoying themselves as they got better with the bow and arrow. Eventually they stopped, and Jennifer had a look around. She expected Caliban to have seen them and join too, especially since he loved archery almost as much as her.

A minute later, Jennifer finally found where Caliban was; him and Leonard were talking with Blockhead, who had a notepad in his hands. He was probably giving them an assignment.

'Excuse me a moment,' the girl told Mark and Blake, then started walking toward Caliban. She wanted to get them all together in order to tell them about what she thought she found out about Blockhead. Luckily, neither Blake nor Mark complained about her leaving all of a sudden.

Before talking to Caliban, she waited for Blockhead to leave so she wouldn't interfere in their business. She noticed that when her trainer turned to walk away and happened to face her, he stared at her in a curious manner, as if he was trying to say something that only she could understand. However, she let the thought slip away and went to talk to Caliban.

'Are you busy?'

'Actually, I am, why?'

'In that case, see you outside after training.'

The boy meant to protest, but Jennifer immediately turned on her heels and went back without giving him the time to respond. When she returned to Mark and Blake, she noticed the confused look on their faces.

'What was that all about?' asked Blake.

'I have to tell you something after training, and I just made sure that Cal would show up.' They stared at her as if she did the most unnatural thing possible. 'It's important.' Eventually, they seemed to understand that she was serious, and didn't complain about it.

Until they got away from training, they practiced everything from brawling to swordsmanship to weightlifting, even Jennifer, as much as her scarring wounds would permit. Finally, they left the training hall and went outside, making a circle as they sat on the grass under the shade of a tree, waiting for Caliban.

'Can't you tell us already?' asked Mark, very anxious to find out what the girl wanted to say.

'No! I already told you, we have to wait for Cal to arrive.'

Ten minutes passed, and still nothing. Caliban was nowhere to be seen, so Jennifer sighed and told them what Blockhead said about having a grey boot knife right after mentioning her bracelet. Apparently, they were unimpressed and thought it a waste of time to gather like that and wait for Caliban who still didn't show up. Blurreydal, however, agreed with the girl's assumption, that their trainer had an alien companion as well, even though it seemed very improbable. After explaining exactly what she thought to be the hidden truth behind Blockhead's words, they finally understood Jennifer's point.

'I told you we could trust him!' pointed out Mark. 'But you wouldn't believe me.' The girl frowned.

'Alright, you were right, but now we have the proof too.'

'What proof?' joined in Blake. 'We still can't be sure that this is true. I'm having a hard time believing it.'

'Fine, that's your opinion, and I won't bother trying to change it. My opinion is that we can almost trust him.' Mark nodded at the girl's words, making Blake frown.

'Just don't do anything stupid thinking he's on our side. You never know. Anyway, I'm going to look for Cal and tell him the news,' Blake said and stood up to leave. Neither Jennifer nor Mark tried to stop him, so they were left on their own.

A few moments of awkward silence passed, until the girl broke the ice and spoke.

'I think that Blockhead could help us, don't you?'

'He *could*, but *would* he?' Mark was being surprisingly cautious, and the girl respected that about him and smiled as she answered.

'Blur once told me that aliens know how to make the right choices. I know he *will* help us if my assumption about the dagger is right. I still have to check though.'

'How do you plan on doing that?' he then asked, very curious to find out. He seemed to agree to the girl's way of thinking this time.

'Blur will help me of course. He can try to talk to this dagger we assume is a transformed alien being, and so we can find out if the assumption is correct.'

'Sounds simple enough.' The boy smiled, so the girl had to smile back. However, their smiles were gone as Mark continued speaking. 'Do you ever get the feeling that you're being watched?' The girl nodded.

'I was thinking the same thing. I'm going back to my room.' Without another word she stood up and left, Mark close behind her.

The boy walked alongside Jennifer until she went inside her room safe and sound, and then went to his own room, where he spent the rest of the evening daydreaming. The girl spent her evening reading those books about spying she got from the Warband Academy.

What neither of them knew and probably wouldn't find out was who the person spying on them was.

As soon as they were out of sight, Caliban jumped down from the tree he had been hiding in. He felt very ashamed for hiding from his own friends. He was set on spending the least amount of time possible with the girl for the time being. In spite of Smolther's request to stop acting so strangely, he refused to listen.

'I wish things didn't have to be so complicated,' he whispered, talking to himself as he started making his way back inside.

Things are simple. You make them complicated.

The boy ignored his alien friend's words and continued walking, sighing every now and then as the image of the girl popped up in his mind without warning. He didn't know it, but the black tattoo on his neck that Smolther formed took the shape of a broken heart.

He walked slowly, barely looking at the surrounding word. Luckily, the other passers-by were careful enough not to bump into him, so he reached his room without harm, despite his carelessness. However, just as he reached for the door knob, someone from behind put his hand on his shoulder, stopping him in his tracks. Caliban turned around and saw none other than Blake, with a worried look.

'What happened to you, Cal? You look like a dead man walking!'

'I'm just tired. I need to be alone for a while.'

'Before that I have something very important to tell you.'

'I already know about Blockhead.' Blake opened his mouth to start telling the news, but then realised what Caliban had just said.

'Wait, you do?'

Without a word, he nodded and turned to open the door. Before Blake woke up from his stupefaction, the door in front of him was already locked shut, and he knew that Caliban wouldn't come back out. He then left, hoping for the best for his confused friend.

28

Alien Intel

Early the following morning, Jennifer made her way towards the training hall. Her goal for the day was to find out what that dagger was all about.

This time when she reached her destination, the training hall wasn't empty. The other person besides her and Blockhead was unmistakably Caliban. He was training with one of the dummies, but to her astonishment he wasn't using a sword, but a dagger. Jennifer suddenly had a flashback from one of the images she saw in the spy manual she read the previous night. However, since the boy hadn't noticed her presence there, she ignored him and went to talk to her trainer.

Check if that dagger really is an alien being, the girl mentally told Blurreydal, who agreed to help.

'You're up early again, Jennifer,' started Blockhead as soon as he noticed her. 'Is there still something troubling you?'

'It seems that Cal woke up even earlier this time,' she whispered, unexplainably disappointed.

'He seems excited about leaving for the Spy Headquarters, and wanted to practice fighting with the dagger.'

'I know that assassins use daggers, and spies need to know how to wield them as well. Swords are forbidden, although I can't understand why.'

'You seem to know quite a lot already, Jennifer! I take it you're passionate about spying also?' The man's reply made the girl smile.

'You have no idea!' she exclaimed, and to her surprise, he let out a faint smile which immediately vanished as soon as it appeared.

You were right, Jenif! Gaever is the alien you said he would be.

'I think,' suddenly said Blockhead after a few moments of silence. He was looking behind the girl, right at Caliban. 'I think you should talk to him. He seems upset about something.'

'I...' The girl hesitated. 'I'm sure I'll have plenty of time for that. When are we leaving anyway?'

'In two days. I was going to tell you today.'

'Two days!' she exclaimed, raising her voice a bit too loud, so she immediately put her hand to her mouth. Then she spoke in a whisper. 'It can't be so soon. Why didn't you tell us earlier?'

'Tell us what?' asked a voice from behind, scaring Jennifer. She turned around to see Caliban, and locked eyes with him for a moment, but he looked away immediately. Blockhead then explained the part which Caliban didn't understand.

'Last night I received a message from one of the leaders at

the Spy Headquarters saying that an escort will arrive for you in two days.'

'But that's so soon!' exclaimed Caliban.

'I know, but I thought you were excited about it. You're not going to back out, are you?'

'Of course not!' protested Caliban, and then the girl whispered, hoping not to be heard, but her words came out crystal clear.

'We have something to do first...'

'What something?' asked their trainer, raising an eyebrow. Just as the girl opened her mouth to explain and confess everything, Caliban was quicker and took the word, leaving Jennifer dumbfounded.

'We know about your *grey dagger*, we really do.' The girl looked with eyes of curiosity, and maybe confusion, because she never got the chance to tell Caliban her theory about the dagger. Even if Blake did, it still wasn't confirmed.

Blockhead on the other hand frowned for a second, as if pondering his words, finding the hidden message behind them. It seemed that he figured out what Caliban meant, because the frown was gone and he put a hand on each of their shoulders, something the two of them found very strange. His words came out as a whisper.

'People are starting to gather and I can't discuss this in public. We'll talk after training, I promise.' The two nodded. Without a word, he waved for them to leave, and so they did without a comment.

A minute later, after they reached the place where Caliban was practicing earlier against the dummies, the girl spoke.

'Did Blake tell you about the grey dagger?' The answer only came after an awkward period of silence, but eventually Caliban spoke, with his head lowered.

'I know there's no point in hiding it, so I'll just say it. I spied on you three yesterday and heard everything. I don't understand what's wrong with me, but I just feel the need to be alone.'

The boy refused to look up, and continued to stare at the floor, and even turned his back to Jennifer. In an attempt to comfort him, she put her hand on his shoulder, but he shook his shoulder free of her hold, so she retreated her arm.

'I'm sorry,' she whispered, not even sure what she was apologising for. When Caliban wouldn't answer, she continued with a sad tone. 'See you after training I hope.'

Immediately she turned and left, jogging her way towards the entrance, where Mark and Blake were just coming in. She tried to fake a happy face, which apparently managed to fool the two boys.

Caliban, however, only seconds after the girl finished speaking, turned around and opened his mouth to apologise for his bizarre behaviour, but she was already far away. In frustration, he kicked the thin air and returned to his dagger training.

How can I be so stupid?!

You have to talk to the girl.

I know, I know. I'll do that, but it's not as simple as it sounds, Smotch!

Why is it hard? You know how to talk. Do you not?

It's not that...

What then?

It's…just forget it.

Hours passed by quicker than expected. Jennifer was anxious to get the chance to talk to Blockhead, as funny as that wish was. She told Mark and Blake the news about their trainer having indeed an alien companion, and they seemed surprised, but suspicious above all else.

This whole time, Caliban stayed on his own, but he always watched Jennifer with the corner of his eye. She never looked his way, apparently busy with her own stuff. Every now and then, he sighed to himself, and Smolther kept trying to encourage him to go talk to her, although in vain.

Finally, people started leaving, but the four kids remained to talk to Blockhead. They all gathered in the same place, and neither of them was late.

She won't even look at me.

Before giving out any information, Blockhead insisted that they go someplace else. 'Even walls have ears,' he told them in a whisper, and walked away as his trainees followed in silence.

As they walked, Caliban stayed behind them, and as soon as Jennifer noticed, she slowed her pace until she was walking alongside him. Now that she tried to look at him, he looked away. 'Sorry,' she whispered as he lowered her head and picked up some speed, but Caliban was still next to her, walking just as fast.

'No, I'm sorry. I don't know what's happening with me these days.'

'Stop blaming yourself for everything, Cal!' The boy gave a long sigh.

'Do you think we can forget about everything and be friends again like we used to be?' he shyly asked, speaking so softly as though he didn't want his words to be heard, much less answered to. However, he relaxed as soon as Jennifer gave him a warm smile.

'Obviously, friends forever.' Caliban smiled back, trying to hide his excitement because they were supposed to focus on the matter at hand, and that was finding out whatever Blockhead had to tell them. 'We'd better catch up with the others,' he suddenly said. Without any warning, Caliban grabbed Jennifer's hand and started jogging until they caught up. He then let go of her hand, and they both acted like that never happened.

It feels like something is missing now...
Her warm hand is full of life, I can feel it.
It really is, Smotch. It really is.

They walked for another minute in silence, until Blockhead reached his destination, and stopped to look at the four anxious trainees.

'My room is sound sealed, so nobody will be able to eavesdrop on us.' The four of them nodded, and followed him inside.

It appeared that Blockhead's room was no bigger than theirs, with just as few places to sit. Having five people crowded in a little room made it feel even smaller.

'Please take a seat, kids,' said the man, motioning toward the bed, apparently the only place where they could sit down. Him, on the other hand remained upright, in front of them.

As soon as they were all settled, he took out a grey knife

from his boot and placed it on the nightstand. To everyone's surprise, it transformed into a miniature human-shaped grey living thing: the alien, Gaever. At the same time, Blurreydal, Smolther and Sangier did the same thing, thus filling up the nightstand in beautiful living colours. The four little aliens seemed busy getting to know each other, and didn't mind the five people who started discussing their own matters.

'You kids are probably wondering how come I got an alien companion of my own, aren't you? I'm not happy that you have so far seen me as the bad guy, but I can't blame you.' Jennifer opened her mouth to protest, but closed it before saying anything because it was true. To her astonishment, the man gave her a warm smile, which looked inappropriate on his forever serious face.

'In that case, I suppose we're on the same team and we're supposed to help each other, right?'

'That's right, Blake.' The kids exchanged a few looks of doubt, but then agreed that they could trust the man before them. Blake took the word once more.

'For as much as we've been told, our alien companions were sent in order to stimulate us into taking action and stopping the war. So far, we've tried to record a message in hope that it would make our leaders realise that this war is pointless.'

Blockhead frowned and looked at each of them in turn. 'Record a message? Give me the details,' he demanded, so Jennifer explained how she had gotten her hands on one of those H4Ks. 'Let me see it.'

Everyone turned to look at Caliban, since he had it. Before anything, he pressed his lips together in doubt, and only with a long moment of hesitation he took out the small device from a pocket and handed it to his trainer who turned it on. They listened to the recording in silence, and at the end Blockhead sighed and spoke.

'Good thing this got to me before you had anyone else see it. I fear you have to delete it because nothing of what you said is applicable.'

'What?' whispered Jennifer, staring at the man who literally just said that all of her work was done in vain.

'I expected you to be lacking important bits of information, but I didn't expect you'd be so serious about taking action so quickly and so efficiently. I can only say I am very proud of your teamwork.'

'But sir, what, then, is all this information we're lacking?' asked Mark. Blockhead frowned and answered. He didn't seem to like reality any more than they did.

'There are things you weren't told, lies that you have all grown up with in hopes to protect you, and your companions respected the authorities' discretion to secrecy and didn't tell you anything. Not even the essentials.' He paused to take a breath and began explaining. The kids' eyes were wide open in utter surprise. 'There are many different alien beings, with their own nations, cultures, mother planets, et cetera, just like us, humans. The species which our alien companions are represented by has for long been our ally, not an enemy. They are quite harmless as you probably noticed. The real enemy is another alien species, which has always tried to take the mother planet of other races. Now they have decided to take over ours by exterminating all living things and starting anew with their own kind. They have done this for thousands of years. War is in their blood and they consider themselves the supreme race, so coming to terms of peace is not an option, unfortunately.'

For a minute, Blockhead stopped talking, and each of the young trainees had a grave look on their face as they absorbed all the new and unexpected information. Questions stirred inside each of them, but only Blake was able to mouth out one of them:

'I still don't get it. Why didn't our companions tell us anything about the truth? Isn't this how *you* found out?'

'They were probably ordered not to tell you when they were sent to us, as you were supposed to find out yourselves. It's your test, if you like. I haven't been raised in this bubble of lies, so I did have a head start. Regardless, I also wanted to mention that I've had Gaever for almost a year, and now we nearly think as one individual. You will understand someday how that feels.' Mark looked down because he felt a strange emptiness stir inside him; he was the only one to not have an alien companion, so he would never understand that feeling Blockhead shared with Gaever.

'What can you tell us about this alien species which is actually our enemy?' asked Blake again. The other three trainees seemed far too busy absorbing all the information to be able to mouth their own thoughts.

'There isn't much to tell. Unlike our companions' species, Yans'ongli, the Huai'ongli have a rather human-like aspect. The main difference is their very large red eyes and their different hair texture. It is much thicker, stronger and sometimes used for more than decorative purposes. They are expected to know how to wield about any object that can cause pain or death, everything from needle pins to lasers. In large, this is about all we know about them.'

The four of them nodded at Blockhead's words, understanding why all that information was hidden from them. If not well prepared and motivated, one could lose his mind when thinking about the strong foes they were up against. It felt like reality retold, finding out so many things about the world they never really knew. The universe suddenly felt big and full of life, not limited anymore to the Academy grounds and its soldiers.

'In that case,' started Mark, preparing to ask the one question everyone was trying to find the answer to. 'Since it's obvious we can't come to peaceful terms with these Huai'ongli, how do we win the war?'

29

Last Memories

'How do we win the war?' repeated Mark when Blockhead remained silent. He seemed to stare into thin air, as if recalling a distant memory.

'We can't outnumber them, and our weapons are no match to theirs. The best solution to defeat them is through sabotage, and for that there are people who infiltrate into their society, passing as one of them. These people make sure to destroy their provisions, weapons, if possible, assassinate some of them, all this while remaining undetected and gathering intel.'

'Sounds like a spy's job...' whispered Jennifer with a smile, and Blockhead nodded. 'But I thought aliens had a different language.'

'Indeed, but as you will soon find out once you get to the Spy Headquarters, there are kind-hearted Huai'ongli who betrayed their own kin in favour of helping us end the war somehow. They are the ones teaching the future spies their language, so they can infiltrate and sabotage.'

'Sounds exciting,' pointed out Caliban. The way he looked at the ceiling with a smile made it obvious he was daydreaming of infiltrating among the Huai'ongli someday. The girl did her best to hold in the giggle, but the smile was inevitable. However, even the smile was gone as Blockhead spoke again, somehow more serious than before.

'This is an extremely dangerous task. Most of the time, the ones appointed for the job sacrifice themselves and do as much as they can to aid in the war, because once they're with the Huai'ongli, it's nearly impossible to get back, even if they don't detect you.'

Caliban and Jennifer's smiles suddenly disappeared, and they both let out a sad 'oh' as they looked at the floor.

'I hope neither of you will ever have to go through that.'

'In other words, you're telling us that we're sitting ducks here, not able to help anyhow?' Blake said suddenly.

'Of course not! Our job here at the Academy is to direct the enemy's eye elsewhere from the real threat, and that is the spy and the assassin. The whole Warband Academy is a huge diversion, and every soldier counts to make this work. So far it has, and at this rate we could win the war and make the Huai'ongli retreat and leave us alone.'

'Hm...' murmured Jennifer. Something was obviously bothering her, so they all turned to look at her in curiosity as she spoke. 'But if the Academy is in their focus, why didn't the Huai'ongli destroy us already? You said they outnumber us and they have better weapons, so what is it that's keeping them away?' For some reason, Blockhead smiled.

'That, my girl, is a very good question. Of course, since improving our strength is pointless, our scientists had mostly been working on tricks to deceive them, hide our location from their sights, and protect us with force barriers if necessary. However, even if they do rediscover our location, there is something they obviously don't like in the surroundings, so they rarely risk an open attack. We still don't know what that thing is, however. I keep wondering if it's the temperature, but it might be something else.'

'There's something I don't understand though,' said Mark. Blockhead let him continue. 'If they already discovered our location once, why do they have to rediscover it? It's not as if the Academy can move.' He seemed truly confused about the matter, and so did the other three trainees as soon as they thought about it. As usual, Blockhead had an answer to anything and everything.

'Here I have to contradict you.' Mark immediately raised an eyebrow in curiosity. 'There is a very large surface of desert around the Academy, past the borders, and this desert's sand can be manipulated enough with underground machinery so that the whole Academy, along with the gates, slowly moves. Because of our camouflage force field, nothing but empty desert can be seen from outside. The Huai'ongli have to risk an attack in order to attempt to rediscover our location.'

Blockhead took a break from explaining, and waited for more questions, but none came.

'I'm quite certain I have given you more than enough to think about,' he smiled. 'As for the H4K, you won't be needing it anymore, so I'll take it back to the lab. It's getting late, you should each get some rest. I don't want to hear any excuses tomorrow morning.'

The four trainees nodded simultaneously, and then stood up. Their alien companions, the Yans'ongli, each came back to them, taking their characteristic shapes. In silence they all left Blockhead's room. As soon as they were out of earshot, Jennifer whispered so that only the boys would hear. 'Well, that was an interesting conversation.'

'So, what now?' asked Blake.

'We should get some rest, it's getting late,' suggested Mark, and everyone agreed, then they started yawning one by one.

'I can't believe we're leaving so soon,' whispered the girl at some point as they were walking. She kept her gaze down to the floor and played with her fingers. She was obviously very nervous. Then she felt an arm wrap around her shoulders, which turned out to be Mark's. She turned to look at him and before she knew it, he kissed her on the forehead. A smile suddenly appeared on her face.

'We're all going to miss you, but if this is the path you want to take, then I'm sure it will turn out well.' Upon hearing Mark's words, her eyes started to feel watery, but she quickly got hold of her emotions and stopped the tears before they showed up.

Without adding anything, they went on walking until the point where they had to split up. 'Good night,' said Blake as he turned the corner with Caliban.

Mark and Jennifer's rooms were in the other direction, so in only a matter of seconds they were left alone in the quiet corridor. The girl was forced to stop walking when Mark stopped and caught her arm gently, so she turned to look at him.

'What's wrong?' she asked, concerned that something bad had happened. The boy hesitated at first as he looked into her eyes, but then spoke.

'It's just...' he started as he let go of her arm. 'I just wish you were staying. It's going to feel very lonely around here without you,' he ended up whispering. Jennifer held her breath for a few moments before speaking. That subject always brought her close to crying.

'You know I'm not changing my mind, Mark. We already talked about this.'

'I know. I just hoped that maybe...maybe you would like to spend a bit more time with me before you go.' The girl watched him in curiosity because she couldn't understand exactly what he wanted. She always spent her time with him. 'Forget it, it was just my ego speaking,' he looked down, ashamed.

The girl patted him on the shoulder. 'No, I really do want to spend more time with you,' she smiled, and all of a sudden Mark's mood lighted up. 'What do you have in mind?'

'Would you care to go for a walk before sleep?' With a smile, the girl nodded and took his hand. Taken aback by her gesture, the boy blushed, but didn't pull away; he was happy.

For minutes they walked hand-in-hand in silence, until Mark decided to start a conversation.

'Do you remember when we first met?' The sudden question made the girl smile.

'How could I forget? I was just five back then. I remember

Blockhead tried to introduce me to so many people, and I was scared of everyone, so I always hid behind him. I think you were the only one I truly allowed myself to talk to. You told me, 'Hi, I'm Mark. You're pretty,' and you lent me your hand to shake.' Mark started laughing as he recalled the memory of innocence.

'And then you took my hand and ran away holding it. Then we started playing like the kids we were. You always laughed about how slow I was, but I never minded because I loved your laugh.'

'I also found it funny that you couldn't climb trees, although you were always taller and stronger than me,' she said, and playfully punched his arm.

'And heavier and slower too. I still can't climb trees like you do.'

'But I can't spar like you do, so it's a tie,' she smiled, and he couldn't help but smile back. Then, he sighed.

'I miss the old days, back when we were so careless about everything. Now just look at us, we're trying to stop a war.' Something about his remark made Jennifer laugh, so he asked her what was so funny.

'*Trying*, well said. We didn't solve anything yet, and probably won't either.'

'Who knows, maybe the day after tomorrow, those new people you will meet will see you as a hero.' Without answering, the girl punched his arm again, this time a little harder. 'Ow, what was that for?'

'I'm no hero,' she laughed.

'You're my hero,' he quickly said, which made the girl

instantly blush. A moment later, she found herself hugging him tightly, acting before her brain could process the movements she was doing. Without a sound, the boy held her close and brushed her hair gently. 'Promise me you'll find a way to be happy no matter what,' he whispered in her ear, but she didn't answer because she started sobbing in silence.

For a few moments there was silence as he allowed her to let out all the negativity she held inside, until she suddenly stopped and pulled away from the hug and looked straight at Mark with bloodshot eyes, a sign that she cried her heart out.

'I'm sorry, I guess I needed to let it all out.' The boy kindly smiled as he took her hand into his.

'Don't worry about it. Let's take you to your room, you could really use some rest, Jen.' Without warning, he picked her up and started walking slowly toward her room. The whole time, Jennifer held her arms wrapped around his neck and leaned her head on his shoulder.

Nobody cares more about you than him, Jenif. I wish you two could stay forever together.

Me too, Blur, but this parting was inevitable. Anyway, it's not like I'll never see him again.

If you say, Jenif.

Not even a minute seemed to pass when Mark stopped and let Jennifer down back on her feet. She smiled and thanked him, to which he answered with a gentle good night kiss on the forehead.

'See you tomorrow,' Jennifer whispered with a blush as she went inside her room.

As soon as she closed the door, she threw herself onto her

bed, somehow more tired than usual. Her thoughts, however, were tireless and shifted from one image to another, mixing up thoughts and ideas endlessly. All the information she discovered that day from Blockhead was a hard hit for her brain.

Blur, why did you never tell me about the Yans'ongli and the Huai'ongli?

I was not allowed. I was told you have to find your own path.

Why did you come here then?

To help you begin to follow your way. I must not interfere in your decisions.

Who forbids you from doing so? the girl then asked, but got no immediate answer, as if Blurreydal needed time to think about the answer.

There is the Cheshei. We must follow him.

Is that your leader?

The Cheshei is not a Yans'ongli. He exists for us only, in us, and sometimes controls us.

So...like a divine power? A god?

I think this is the word in the humane language...a god.

The girl stopped answering because she was exhausted, and before she knew it, she fell into unconsciousness, into a dreamless sleep. All the foreign information was still stirring inside her head, but somehow it all became clear as she woke up the next morning, full of energy. Jennifer had a feeling that something was missing, or would be missing.

Then she remembered it was her last day at the Warband Academy.

30

The Final Day

At breakfast, the girl met up with her friends. Somehow, everyone was there: Mark, Caliban and Blake. To make things even stranger, Caliban seemed exhausted, something rather abnormal for him in the morning.

'What's up with you, Cal?' asked Mark as he patted him on the shoulder.

'Couldn't sleep,' he answered shortly. The only emotion shown on his face was exhaustion.

'Something bothering you?' then asked Blake. After a moment of hesitation, Caliban nodded, to everyone's surprise. 'What is it?'

'It's about what Blockhead told us. I stayed up all night thinking...' he started, but then his eyes closed and he stopped talking for a bit. He held his head in his hands, but it almost fell and hit the table. He then opened his eyes when Mark shook him gently. 'I was thinking... The Yans'ongli are our allies, but if there are so many alien species, why don't we try to get more allies?' He spoke in one breath, and then let out an audible sigh and let his head rest on the table.

'I'll bring you some coffee,' said the girl as she stood up and left.

The three boys remained silent for a bit. Caliban wasn't moving, and seemed to finally relax as Mark and Blake looked at each other as if they were trying to talk telepathically. Then they finally spoke, but in a low voice so as to not bother Caliban.

'He has a point,' started Blake, and Mark nodded.

'We should ask Blockhead about it. I doubt he hasn't thought of it before, so I'm wondering what the explanation could be.'

Before Blake had time to add anything, Caliban murmured a 'mmm' in agreement. Just then, Jennifer returned with a cup of coffee, smiling.

'This should help,' she said, as she put the cup on the table. Mark gently shook Caliban's shoulder again, and he then got back up, his eyes drooping evermore. As soon as he noticed the cup of coffee in front of him, he had a long sip, which apparently woke him instantly.

'Ah! It's burning!' he shouted. The girl laughed as Mark and Blake stared in confusion.

'Of course it's hot, what did you expect?' Moments later Caliban finally calmed down, and couldn't help but frown. 'Look at the bright side, it woke you up,' she continued with an awkward smile. It didn't make Caliban any happier, however.

'Maybe we should get going,' suggested Blake. Mark agreed, and they were the first ones to stand up.

'You guys go ahead. I'll catch up after I finish my coffee.'

Jennifer was the last to stand up, and with only a nod, turned and left with the other two boys. On the way, she spoke.

'I hope Blockhead has time to talk with us today too. I really want to know more about all of this.' The boys simply nodded and continued to walk silently.

As soon as they reached the Training Hall, they noticed Blockhead approaching them in a hurry. As soon as he was close enough, he whispered for only them to hear.

'See you again after training.' Without wasting another second, he turned and left. Although confused, the three trainees were glad they sorted that out, and could now focus on training. The last training day in the Warband Academy.

'Since it's my last day here, what do you guys think I should do today?' asked the girl. Mark and Blake took a moment to think, until one of them finally spoke.

'Maybe you should practice archery, since you mentioned you'd be needing it,' suggested Blake, but the girl shook her head.

'I'm full of energy, I need something that involves more movement. Like running.' As she spoke, she started jumping in place a little so as to show she couldn't just sit in one place. It made Mark laugh.

'How about a race then? First to circle around the hall twice is the better sprinter.'

'Sounds good to me. Blake, you in?' As he answered negatively, he shrugged. 'Okay then. Mark, I'll give you a head start,' she winked at him.

'Fine, but promise me you won't ask Blurreydal for extra strength.' Before answering the girl laughed.

'I don't need Blur to win this. Blake, give us the start if you'd please.'

'Sure. Ready, set, Mark go!' Without hesitation, Mark started sprinting along the wall of the Training hall. Ten seconds later he told Jennifer to start, and before he knew it, she had already disappeared from his sight.

As the two of them sprinted, Blake just watched. Not even a minute passed, and they were finishing the first lap, shoulder to shoulder. At some point, Mark leaned toward Jennifer so as to push her to the side to slow her down, but his attempt failed as she slightly slowed her pace on purpose and got behind Mark, who was now trying to regain his balance.

Blake focused all his attention on the race, so he jumped in surprise when he felt a hand on his shoulder coming from behind. He immediately turned around, ready to defend himself, when he saw Caliban and relaxed.

'So, what did I miss?' he asked. The coffee seemed to have had a visible effect on Caliban, because he seemed almost full of life.

'Those two are racing,' answered Blake as he pointed to the place they were currently at. 'I think Mark's going to win.'

'I vote for Jennifer. She doesn't seem half as tired as Mark is right now. Still, I'm surprised they're keeping the same speed.'

'You're right, Jennifer is usually faster than that.'

'She's obviously letting him win. How nice of her!' exclaimed Caliban as he faintly smiled, watching the girl run.

She didn't seem to strain herself almost at all; she was a natural sprinter.

Seconds later, they finished their race, and Mark seemed to have been first. As they gasped for air, they seemed to be very joyful, recalling childhood memories.

I wish she could smile like that more often, thought Caliban, but his thoughts were immediately interrupted as Blake shook his shoulder with power.

'Stop staring,' he whispered. With wide eyes, Caliban turned to look at the boy who still had his hand on his shoulder. 'It's not polite you know.'

'Uh...I'm sorry.'

With a smile and a pat on the shoulder, Blake immediately changed the subject.

'We'll be meeting Blockhead again today by the way.' At hearing the news, Caliban sketched a tired smile. Then without warning, Blake walked toward the two sprinters, so Caliban followed.

'That was an impressive race!'

'Thanks...Blake,' said Mark in between breaths. 'So,' he then added. 'What's next?'

For the rest of the day until training was over, the four of them spent some time sword fighting. Caliban insisted on trying to use a dagger instead of a common sword, so Jennifer did so too. It turned out that Caliban could use it naturally, while Jennifer could barely understand how to attack with it. It made her feel exposed somehow.

Eventually, people started to leave, and when everyone was gone, the four trainees went with Blockhead to his room just like the previous day so they could talk in private.

Once they were all gathered up like the day before, Caliban was the first to speak, apparently very anxious to find out more details about everything.

'Sir, you told us there are many alien species, right?' He nodded in response, probably expecting the question that was coming. 'Then how come we only have the Yans'ongli as allies?'

'This is a delicate matter, Caliban, but this is a good question worth a good answer. As you probably know, alliances involve paying a tribute, and unfortunately for us, the tribute that we would have to pay to most alien species is far too much for us to handle. The Yans'ongli were the only ones willing to accept an alliance, and that is not at an exchange of goods.'

'What did they ask for then?' asked Jennifer, keeping an eye on their alien companions who were all gathered together in their normal shapes.

'They asked for a bond between our races.'

'A bond?' asked Mark, and Blockhead nodded, but explained no further. Without much thought, Mark understood that the bond was between the human and his alien companion, just like Jennifer and Blurreydal, or Blake and Sangier. Realising he was the only one without an alien companion, he sighed. 'It must be nice,' he whispered, but brought no reaction to anyone.

'Do you have any more questions?' asked Blockhead, and after a few seconds of silence, the trainees shrugged, unable to think of anything more to ask at that moment. 'Good. I brought you here because I needed to discuss something else with you. It's about the way things are going to change for you starting with tomorrow.'

The four of them remained silent. It was obvious that it was a very delicate subject, something they would've rather avoided talking about. Still, they knew it was inevitable now, so they continued to listen to their trainer's words.

'I expect you, Caliban and Jennifer, to be up especially early. Come to the main entrance of the Academy. There is something I need to warn you about though, something you might find shocking at first. The person coming to pick you up is a woman.'

'A woman?' asked Jennifer, unsure if she heard it right. She accepted the fact that there were probably hundreds of alien species in the galaxy, but hearing that there were more human females like her seemed unreal. 'Why?' she then whispered. Her complete question was actually 'why am I the only girl here?' Luckily, Blockhead understood the meaning behind her one-word question and answered.

'The explanation is quite simple. Women were never ones to go to war, and instead remained in the shadows, hidden and protected from the enemy, helping in an indirect way if at all. You, however, were born in one of the very few families where the mother was a warrior just as much as the father.'

'Why did I never know of this? Where are my parents? *Who* are they?'

Before answering, Blockhead let out a little laugh, as if he found her shock funny. The other boys only stared in wonder, apparently unable to process the information.

'I swore an oath not to tell you, but I have faith that you will find out yourself soon enough. Still, bear in mind this: your parents are alive, and have and always will watch over you. At least one of them. You just don't know it yet.'

The girl remained silent for a while. She had no idea how she was supposed to react to this bit of information, so all the confusion ended up with her not reacting anyhow.

'Anyway,' continued Blockhead. 'Back to the point. Don't act too surprised if you see several girls at the Spy Headquarters. There are only a few, but still enough for it to seem a shock to you. This much was for you two, future spies. As for Mark and Blake,' he said as he turned his gaze toward them, 'don't expect any changes regarding training.'

The two boys nodded. It was obvious that things wouldn't change for them. When none would react, Blockhead continued.

'And one last thing before you go.' He turned to look at the to-be spies. 'The leaders at the Spy Headquarters do know about the Yans'ongli, but the trainees most probably don't. Keep it a secret there as you kept it here. If you happen to detect people with alien companions, then you know you can trust them.' As he finished, Blockhead winked, then told them to enjoy their evening.

Until it got dark, the four of them had a walk outside. They were mostly silent because they were all thoughtful.

Mark was obviously wondering how lonely the Warband Academy was going to seem without the girl always there to cheer him up. Caliban was daydreaming that one day he would have the opportunity of infiltrating among the Huai'ongli, although at the risk of his own life. Blake was thinking about Caliban's idea, that maybe there were more alien species which could eventually become their allies; he knew he simply had to do more research on the topic. Jennifer, however, kept staring at the slowly darkening sky.

'What are you thinking about?' asked Mark in a low voice, and the girl's answer came just as softly.

'I was wondering...how big is this world after all? Up to now, the limits reached no more than the Academy grounds, and suddenly this world expanded to a whole universe. I can't be sure, but it sounds like a huge thing to me...without limits. It's all so sudden...'

'You're actually thinking of your parents, aren't you?' The girl nodded in response, but keeping her eyes on the stars that were starting to show up one by one.

'I'm sure they're somewhere out there, but even if I meet them, how will I know they're my parents? I've never seen them. I don't even have a clue on their whereabouts.'

In an attempt to comfort her, Mark patted her on the shoulder when Blake interrupted.

'Guys, it's getting dark so we'd better go back inside.' Everyone agreed without comment.

They made their way back to their rooms in almost complete silence, making sure to say goodbye in case they wouldn't have the chance to do so in the morning.

A dreamless sleep soon took each of them, and morning arrived before they knew it.

A new life was just starting.

Epilogue

Early morning, so early that not even the sun was to be seen, the Warband Academy's gates opened to let in a pale orange carriage driven by two golden horses.

The two horses came to a halt as they met Blockhead, who showed no emotion. Behind him, however, stood the one girl who was to leave, and the one boy who would accompany her: Jennifer and Caliban. They stood still and silent as they watched how the carriage's movement slowed to a stop. Their faces showed obvious curiosity, a sense of fear, and their drooping eyes showed that they hadn't slept well that night. Their eyes were fighting to stay open, and they never seemed to look elsewhere but toward the slowing carriage.

From behind came another, ruining the perpetual silence which barely lasted a few moments, but seemed somehow endless to those waiting. The young man who was approaching didn't say a word, however, he laid his hand on the girl's shoulder. He then leaned closer to whisper in her ear:

'I'll miss you.'

'I'll never forget you, Mark. I wish to see you again soon,' she whispered, always watching the carriage along with Caliban.

The door then opened, and out came a thin, tall figure wearing black clothes and a black hooded cloak, shadowing the face. At the waist there was a thin belt holding several knives, obviously for throwing, and on the other side there was a dagger. Even the trousers had sockets for more knives, and the shirt was padded with several layers of thick leather.

This woman was the person they knew was coming. Maybe it was the fact that Blockhead had mentioned it, or the way she moved as graceful as a stalking predator, or just her thin body that gave away the fact that there was no man hiding in the shadow of the cloak. Jennifer knew undoubtedly that it was *her*. Something about her felt strangely familiar, but she couldn't put her finger on it, thus letting the thought slip away.

The woman approached Blockhead in silence, her footsteps making absolutely no sound as she walked. A moment of silence reigned even after she froze in place. She looked up to Blockhead; even as she was tall, he was still half a head taller than her. She wouldn't speak first as far as it seemed.

'Camryn.'

'Breightad.'

'Good to see you are well.'

'You know we don't have time for pleasantries.' The man lowered his head as if those firm words drained him. 'The shield will only last for a couple more hours. We need to return before noon.' The man then nodded and turned ninety degrees to the side to look at the waiting trainees from behind. They approached in silence. Mark remained behind, watching his friends leave him, possibly forever.

'Jennifer, Caliban, this is Camryn from the Spy Headquarters. I leave you under her care. Respect and listen to her as you did to me. Farewell.'

Before leaving with the woman, the two trainees bowed shortly and followed inside the carriage. The girl threw one last glance toward her childhood friend, only to see him smiling. She knew how much it pained him to smile at a moment like that so she wanted to return the favour, but before she gained control of all those tired facial muscles, it was already too late. She was inside the carriage.

As soon as the door closed behind her, they started moving, first at a slow speed, and then faster and faster. With every passing moment they grew more distant to the world they had known so far, and closer to the one that was just beginning.

Back at the Academy, both Blockhead and Mark stared in silence at the closing gates, searching for another glimpse of the disappearing carriage. However, it seemed to turn invisible as soon as it reached the desert wasteland outside the Academy's boundaries. They both had tears flooding their eyes, tears that couldn't be held in.

'There goes my girl,' whispered Blockhead, not knowing that Mark heard his words, although he wouldn't show it.

Without warning, the sun was finally rising on the clear sky, bringing a new day along with a whole new life.